BOOK ONE

Tig Ripley, Rock 'n' Roll Rebel

Text copyright © 2016 Ginger Rue

Cover illustration by Amanda Haley

Sleeping Bear Press™

2395 South Huron Parkway, Suite 200, Ann Arbor, MI 48104
www.sleepingbearpress.com
© Sleeping Bear Press

Printed and bound in the United States.
10 9 8 7 6 5 4 3 2 1

Library of Congress Cataloging-in-Publication Data
Names: Rue, Ginger, author.
Title: Rock 'n' roll rebel / written by Ginger Rue.
Description: Ann Arbor, MI : Sleeping Bear Press, [2016]
Series: Tig Ripley; book 1 | Summary: Looking to propel her into
the spotlight at her middle school, thirteen-year-old Tig Ripley
starts an all-girl rock band with her cousin and two school friends.
Identifiers: LCCN 2016007658
ISBN 9781585369454 (hard cover)
ISBN 9781585369461 (paper back)
Subjects: | CYAC: Rock groups--Fiction. | Popularity--Fiction.
Middle schools--Fiction. | Schools--Fiction. | Self-perception--Fiction.
Classification: LCC PZ7.R88512 Ro 2016 | DDC [Fic]--dc23
LC record available at https://lccn.loc.gov/2016007658

For the Orbits, who never made a record or sold out a concert hall,
but whose drummer is still one of my all-time favorites.
I love you, Daddy!

Tig Ripley

Rock 'n' Roll Rebel

★ GINGER RUE ★

PUBLISHED BY SLEEPING BEAR PRESS

Chapter One

On the long list of reasons why Tig Ripley shouldn't have set out to form an all-girl rock band, probably the biggest was the fact that she couldn't play an instrument or even sing particularly well.

But Tig had never been one to let details interfere with her plans.

After all, there were so many good reasons to do it—like major middle-school street cred, for one. If she were in a band—and the leader of it, no less—she'd cease to be a background extra in the drama that was Lakeview Heights Middle School.

She'd become the leading lady, and girls like Regan Hoffman, with their sixth sense of exactly how many bangle bracelets to stack per arm and when to put a belt with a dress for a touch of I-just-threw-this-together—well, they'd just be gnats on an Alabama summer night. Who could compete with a girl who plays drums?

But the real catalyst behind Tig's interest in playing drums? Truth was, it had a lot to do with Will Mason.

No, Will Mason wasn't some dreamy, unattainable guy Tig barely knew but had been pining away for since he'd accidentally brushed up against her in the hall or asked to borrow a pencil. Hardly. What Will lacked in dreaminess, he more than made up for in annoyingness. One might have said Tig and Will were friends . . . except for the fact that she couldn't stand him. They sat at the same lunch table, but that was more a function of their having the same social status (basically none) and the same circle of friends—the pretty-smart B students who could have probably made As if they cared enough to try.

Will played drums in the school band and carried sticks in his back pocket at all times. Tig felt that Will thought this made him cool, so one day when he began teasing her about her hair, her braces, or one of the other billion things he picked on her about, she decided to set him straight.

"Let me guess: you're so into your music that you can't be without your drumsticks for even a moment?" she asked. "Or do you just want everyone to know you're a drummer because that's, you know, *such* a big deal?"

"I suppose you think you could play the drums, Antigone," he countered.

Tig's first name was Greek and pronounced *Ann-TIG-ah-nee*, but Will liked to pronounce it *AN-ti-gone*, as in, "against going away."

"I'm sure I could if I felt like it," Tig said.

"Yeah, right. Girls don't play the drums."

Of all the guys to get stuck next to at lunch. Will always sat at the end of the adjoining table of his best friend, Sam, so Will and Tig usually ended up elbow to elbow.

"Um, 1960 called," she said. "They want their male chauvinism back. What, you think girls aren't strong enough to beat two puny little sticks against a circle? Or we're afraid we might break a nail?"

Will scoffed. "It's not an issue of physical strength. It's an issue of leadership. Drummers set the pace. The whole band depends on them for the beat."

"You're actually saying a girl couldn't lead a band?" Tig asked.

"The truth hurts."

"For your information, if you can learn how to play the drums, it can't be that hard. I could probably get in a band before you could."

"Maybe," he said, trying to sound like he wasn't riled. "It's good business to throw a good-looking chick in a rock band. Probably get more gigs that way."

Although Tig was a little thrown by the "good-looking chick" comment (did Will think she was good-looking?), she was more focused on his ridiculous arrogance. Like he knew anything about business or gigs. Did he not realize he was thirteen, like nearly everyone else in their class? "I suppose you're speaking from your vast gigging experience in the band room, playing snare with a metronome?"

"Haters gonna hate," he said.

"And furthermore, you assume that bands are made up of guys."

"They are."

"Ever hear of the Go-Go's?"

"I think you just made my point. The only girl band you can think of is from, like, thirty years ago. And besides, the only reason you know who they are is because you saw their documentary on VH1 about how they crashed and burned. Girl bands are gimmicks. They don't work."

"How would you know?"

"Because girls can't get along, period, much less keep a band together. Girls are too jealous of other girls. They can't trust one another."

"Will, you're such a doofus," said Kyra, who'd been half listening while drinking her water.

Somebody else at the table changed the subject, and that was that.

Except that it wasn't.

Because when Tig got home, she called Big Daddy. "I want to learn how to play the drums," she told him.

Chapter Two

Back in the sixties, Tig's grandfather had been a drummer in a band called the Orbits. It was Big Daddy and his best friend, Jerry, and a couple of other guys. The lead singer had been a guy named Danny Speed. Big Daddy swore that was the singer's real name, even though it sounded made-up. The Orbits had broken up when Big Daddy and Jerry had enlisted in the navy, and nobody knew what happened to Danny Speed, though Tig liked to think he'd been really handsome and had moved to somewhere cool, like California.

In any case, Big Daddy hadn't played drums in

years and had sold his set decades ago. But as the oldest grandchild on her dad's side of the family, Tig was the apple of her grandfather's eye. So he wasted no time after Tig's phone call and went out and bought her a respectable but reasonably priced drum set.

They set up the drum kit in the green house, which wasn't a greenhouse as in a place where you grow stuff, but an actual green-painted house built from cement blocks. It had been the "mother-in-law apartment" for the former owners of the house Tig shared with her parents and younger sister and brother. It had one main room, a bathroom, and a closet, and they'd used it only for storage up until that point. Tig's mom was happy to put the drums in there instead of the main house, since Tig's younger sibs already made enough noise for anybody.

"It must be in the genes," BD said when he finally got the drum kit all set up. "Going to be a drummer like your old BD!"

Tig had stopped calling her grandfather Big Daddy a year or so ago, thinking BD sounded less babyish.

"Yes, sir. Hey, BD, how long do you think it'll be before I can play a full song? A couple of weeks, maybe?"

BD laughed. "Maybe a little longer than that. It takes coordination. Kind of like 'rub your head, pat your tummy.'"

After only one lesson with BD the Monday after he assembled the drum kit, Tig was almost ready to give up. "This is way worse than trying to rub your head and pat your tummy," she told him. "It's more like 'rub your head, pat your tummy, kickbox, and juggle knives.'"

"You need a real teacher," he said. "You'll do better with a stranger, someone you'll be too embarrassed to disappoint."

So Tig met her new drum teacher, Lee, at the local music store the following Friday afternoon. He taught her the names of each drum in the kit: the bass was the one on the floor played with her right foot, the snare was the main drum, and the others were called toms — the high tom, the middle tom, and the floor tom. The cymbals were called the ride, the crash, and the hi-hat.

Lee said she would use the hi-hat most often, at least at first.

"Everything with drums is basically looking for the booms and the chicks," Lee told her. Tig thought it sounded like some sort of slang for "boys and girls." But then Lee put on some music with a distinctive drumbeat: the Rolling Stones' "Honky Tonk Women."

"This is way before your time—and even way before mine, but the drum intro is great, and it's slow enough that you can kind of pick out what's going on," Lee explained.

After he played the song's intro a few times on his phone, boosted through the speakers in the lesson room, Lee sat down and played along on his electronic drum kit. Tig noticed that the bass drum pedal seemed to be moving quite a bit, even on this kind of slow song. She couldn't always tell which was an actual kick of the drum pedal and which were vibrations from the pedal having been kicked, but it looked cool. She couldn't wait until she could do that. Lee handed her a drumstick and let Tig hit the snare every time there was a chick. It was fun, and Tig couldn't help but feel pleased with herself that she could now differentiate between a boom and a chick. She felt proud to have learned something from the very first lesson. Things were a bit harder at home when she tried doing both the booms and the chicks by herself for her practice exercises, but Lee assured her it would just take some getting used to.

He taught her all the basic drum fills—patterns played with the sticks—and flams, which were a little bit trickier because they were patterns that involved letting the stick bounce instead of deliberately hitting it.

As frustrating as it was to practice the same fills and flams over and over and over with varying levels of success, Tig felt cool playing the drums. Powerful. Hitting the bass drum with force so that she could feel the boom all the way in her stomach went against everything she'd ever been taught about being a proper Southern young lady.

She wondered why she hadn't started a long time ago.

Chapter Three

"**Y**ou've got to learn how to play bass," Tig told Kyra on the phone after she'd had three once-a-week drum lessons.

"What? Why?"

"So you can be in my band," Tig replied.

"What band? When did you join a band?"

"I didn't. That's why I need you to learn bass, so I can form one."

There was no way Tig could do something as monumental as forming a band without including Kyra. They were first cousins and had been joined at the hip since birth. Tig's mom and Kyra's dad were sister and brother, and the Bennett family was tight. Even when Tig and Kyra did get mad at each other, they had little choice but to make up or endure infinitely awkward family gatherings.

"Why bass?" Kyra asked. "Why not guitar?"

"Because bass players look cool," Tig said. "You don't have to really move a lot, so you get to have this kind of I'm-so-bored-with-being-a-rock-star-that-I-could-fall-asleep thing going on onstage. Totally cool."

The real reason Tig had chosen bass for Kyra was because Lee had told her it was the easiest instrument to choose from. "The guitar requires a sizable amount of fine motor skills, of dexterity," Lee had said. And while Kyra was many things, dexterous wasn't one of them. Kyra's dad had nicknamed Kyra "Grace" when she was little because she was always running into stationary objects.

Pretty much anybody can walk a bass line, Lee had said.

"I don't know," Kyra said. "I'm not really musically inclined."

"Come on," Tig replied. "Pretty much anybody can walk a bass line." She said it as if she knew what it meant.

"Well, it might be fun to be in a band," Kyra said.

"It'll be awesome. It's, like, we'll, you know . . . matter."

"We could be popular!" Kyra's pitch went up a full octave.

"It's not about that," Tig said with a sigh. One thing Kyra and Tig did not have in common: Kyra desperately wanted to be in with the Regan Hoffman crowd, while Tig . . . Well, it was more like she wanted to prove to the Regan Hoffmans of the world how little she cared about them. She wanted to transcend them. While Kyra dreamed of sitting at Regan's lunch table, Tig fantasized about being *invited* to sit at Regan's lunch table only to refuse the invitation. *That*, she had tried several times to explain to Kyra, would be the height of cool, but Kyra wouldn't buy it. She couldn't fathom why anyone wouldn't want to be popular.

"So, look, are you going to do it or not?" Tig asked.

"All right," Kyra said. "But where are you going to get the other musicians?"

Kyra had a point. Tig didn't really know how she would go about finding the other band members, but she didn't want to admit that to Kyra and make it seem like she didn't have it all figured out.

"Simple," Tig said. "Auditions."

"Auditions?" Kyra asked. "Where? Who? When?"

"You forgot what, how, and why," Tig said. "Look, I'll put up a sign on the bulletin board in the music store. We can have a cattle call audition."

"At the school auditorium?"

No way, Tig thought. She didn't want Will or anyone else at school to know about the band until they were formed and actually good. "How about at your church building? They have a stage there."

"I could probably set that up, I guess," Kyra said.

"Then it's settled. We'll have auditions a week from tomorrow."

Chapter Four

A week and a day later Tig and Kyra sat in the small auditorium of Kyra's church building downtown. They both had clipboards, although neither was sure what they were supposed to do with them.

"No one's going to show up," Kyra said.

"Sure they will," Tig said. "You're always saying to think positively."

"Okay. I'm positive no one's going to show up."

"Very funny," Tig said. She was just about to start playing a game on her phone when someone walked through the doorway.

It was a guy. A high-school guy.

A cute high-school guy.

With a guitar.

"Is this the place for the auditions?" he asked. He had blond hair that fell over his forehead. He was broad-shouldered and had perfectly white, straight teeth.

"*Yes!*" Kyra said. "Come right in!"

Tig cleared her throat. "What she means is . . . this is the place for the auditions for the *all-girl* band." Tig held up a copy of the flyer she'd posted in the music store.

"Yeah," he said. "I was thinking maybe that was optional?"

"Totally optional," Kyra said.

"No, it's not," Tig said.

"Tig!" Kyra whispered a little too loudly. "Are you *blind*? He's gorgeous!"

"He's also a guy," Tig replied.

"Precisely my point!"

"I'm sorry," Tig said. "But this really is for girls only. Thanks for coming, though."

"Worth a shot," the guy said.

"Call me!" Kyra yelled just as the door closed behind him.

" 'Call me'?" Tig asked. " 'Call me'? Call you what, *desperate*?"

"You're out of your mind!" Kyra said. "We could've had Mr. Hottie McHotterson in our band! Hours and hours of practice together!"

"Oh, Kyra, he's way too old for you. He's probably at least sixteen."

"So? He could wait for me."

"Yeah. Right."

Before they could say any more, the door opened again. This time it was a girl.

She looked to be about the right age, and basically normal.

Except for the fact that she was carrying an accordion.

"Hi!" she said. "I'm here for the audition for the band!" She walked to the stage and pulled her accordion wide as though it were taking a deep breath.

"Um, we're actually not . . . ," Kyra began. But it was too late. The girl launched right in and began playing something.

"She's not half bad," Tig said to Kyra.

"But it's an accordion!" Kyra said. "We can't have an accordion in our band!"

Tig had to agree. With an inexperienced band, an accordion would be quirky at best and ridiculously dorky at worst. Tig waved her hand, and the girl stopped playing. "That was really nice," Tig said. "But I'm afraid we're not exactly in the market for an accordion player. Thanks anyway."

The girl came down from the stage and pulled up a chair next to Tig. Right next to her. Uncomfortably close. "But I can play anything you want," she said. "Rock, polka, classical, jazz . . ."

"Accordion jazz?" Tig asked. "That's a new one."

Kyra bumped her with her elbow.

"But as I said, we're not looking for an accordion player."

"A lot of people don't realize how versatile an

instrument the accordion is," the girl said. She launched into a history of the accordion, none of which Tig actually heard because she was too busy noticing that the girl had begun picking a scab on her arm. *Tig's* arm.

Tig moved her arm away. "What are you doing?"

"I was telling you about the rich history of the accordion," she replied.

"No, I mean, why were you picking my arm?"

"Oh, sorry. I like to pick things."

"Maybe you should've played the banjo," Kyra said.

"Anyway," Tig said. "Thanks for coming, and it was nice to meet you."

"Your loss," said the accordion player.

When she was gone, a voice from the back of the room said, "Yo, that was just sad." Tig and Kyra turned to see a heavyset redheaded girl wearing a County T-shirt. She must have come through the other doorway. "Ready for a real audition?" the girl said. She walked up to the stage area.

"What's your instrument?" Tig asked.

"Yo, got my instrument right here," the girl said,

pointing to her throat. "Check it out: Edgy Abz in the house." Then she launched into a lengthy rap. It went so fast, Tig couldn't make out everything, but she was able to determine that it involved a car chase from the authorities.

"Okay," Tig said when the rap was finished. "How about that."

"What's your name again?" Kyra asked.

"Edgy Abz," she replied. "With a z."

"Your parents named you that?" said Kyra.

"Abby," she said. "But yo, that's wack."

"Well, Edgy . . . ," Tig began. "Um, Abby . . . Abz. . . ." Tig wasn't sure what to call her. Miss Abz? "That was very impressive."

"So when do I start?" asked Miss Abz.

"Oh," Tig said. "We actually aren't looking for . . . someone with your particular skill set."

"You frontin'?" asked Abz.

"I don't know," Kyra said. She turned to Tig. "Are we frontin'? What does that mean?"

"I don't know," Tig replied. Then to Abz she said,

"No offense. You're a really good rapper. We just don't need one."

"You buckin' me? I spit some throwed flow, stuntin' up in here."

"Whoa, set the ket, homegirl," Kyra said.

Tig looked at her like she'd just sprouted a unicorn's horn. "What does that even mean?" she whispered.

Kyra shrugged. "I saw it on TV once."

"What my associate means," Tig said to Abz, "is that while we deeply admire your talent, we're more of a traditional rock kind of band. But we really appreciate your coming out today and sharing your talent with us. And if we hear of any bands who need someone with your skills, which are, as we mentioned, extremely impressive, we will certainly recommend you." Abz stared at them. "Wholeheartedly recommend you," Tig said. "That's what we will do."

Abz's face was as red as her hair. "You gig, I'll be there," she said. "To burn you to the ground."

As Abz stomped away, Kyra yelled after her, "Peace out?" but there was no reply.

"That went well," Tig said sarcastically. "I guess we're all out of auditioners."

"What are we going to do now?" Kyra said. "This was a total bust."

"I'll think of something," Tig said. "But let's just keep this to ourselves."

"You mean this horrible audition exercise that was a complete disaster? Oh, I'm just *dying* to tell everyone about this."

"Well, obviously that," Tig said. "But I mean the whole band thing in general. Tell no one at school about it. No one. Got it?"

"Why not? Why can't we tell people we're starting a band?"

"Because after this, I don't want any more volunteers," Tig said. "I'd rather recruit. You know, I've been thinking—Olivia took piano lessons for, like, a zillion years before she got so involved with tennis. Maybe she could play the keyboard?"

"We could ask her," Kyra said.

"Leave that to me," Tig replied. "I don't want it

out on the grapevine that we're looking. I want to hand-select our members. Besides, we need to wait a little longer until you and I have had time to learn our instruments better before we add anyone else. So don't tell anyone about the band. Got it?"

"I'm not going to tell anybody." Kyra rolled her eyes.

"I'm not kidding around," Tig said. "You're about as good at secret keeping as you were at the violin. Or baton twirling. Or French. Or—"

"That's not fair! Name one time I haven't kept a secret!"

"Hello? Michael Hart? Fifth grade? You told him I was in love with him?"

"Well, you were."

"But he didn't have to know that!"

"It slipped out!" Kyra said.

" 'It slipped out.' Was that your mantra in that ill-fated yoga class you took? Because you say it enough. Like the time when—"

"Okay, okay," said Kyra. "I got it. I promise. I won't tell a soul."

Chapter Five

Kyra was true to her word.

For about two weeks.

And for Kyra, that was pretty amazing. Tig was so impressed by how long it had taken Kyra to spill the beans, she almost wasn't mad.

Problem was, of all the people to tell, Kyra had chosen Haley Thornton.

"No, you did not," Tig said as they stood at their lockers before school. The tone of disbelief was almost genuine. "Haley Thornton, really? Of all people . . ."

"What's wrong with Haley?" Kyra asked. "I thought

it was Regan you didn't like."

"Kyra, don't you get it? Haley is almost worse than Regan."

"What do you mean?

"I mean that at least Regan rarely bothers with tormenting the little people like us most of the time. But Haley . . . Well, Haley's a sidekick, and sidekicks always need to up the ante in some way to stay relevant. It's Haley's job to mock and degrade other people to amuse Regan; it's Regan's job to be amused. They're like the court jester and the queen."

"Oh, come on, Tig. Don't you think you're being just a bit dramatic?"

"No, I don't. And why did you tell her about the band, anyway? You weren't supposed to tell anyone. You promised!"

"Tig, don't be mad."

Tig sighed. "I guess what's done is done. Just forget about it." She slammed her locker door.

"As long as you're forgiving me," Kyra said, "there is just one other little thing."

"What?"

"I kind of asked her to be the lead singer."

"You *what?*"

"Well, she's a really good singer, right?" Kyra replied. "I mean, she played Lucy in *You're a Good Man, Charlie Brown* this past summer."

"Did you see her in the show?"

"No."

"Then how do you know she's a good singer?" Tig asked.

"Well, did you see her in the show?"

"No," Tig said.

"Then how do you know she's not?"

"Look, a part in a local theater production doesn't mean squat. For all you know, they gave her the part because her dad's office was sponsoring the production or something. Or even if she does sing on key, singing in musical theater isn't the same as fronting a rock band. You have to have a rock 'n' roll kind of voice, plus that certain . . . charisma."

"Haley has charisma," Kyra said. "She's super-popular."

"That doesn't mean she's got charisma. That means she's a Bot with the right brand of jeans."

"Come on, Tig. . . ."

"The fact of the matter is, you had no right—none!—to invite Haley or anyone else to be the lead singer! It's not your band."

"I thought it was our band, together," Kyra said.

Once again Tig sighed. "Don't make the puppy dog eyes." Kyra whimpered, which almost made Tig laugh. Almost. "All right. I guess we can give her a chance."

"You're the best!" Kyra squealed. Then she said in a conspiratorial whisper, "Tig, if Haley is our lead singer, that means she'll be hanging out with us, and if she's hanging out with us, we'll probably all start going to the same parties and having sleepovers and scheduling our classes together, and the next thing you know, we'll be *in*!"

"How many times do I have to tell you that I have zero desire to 'be in'? I'd rather gargle acid."

"You say that, but once we're in, you'll change your

mind. Besides, somebody with Haley's social connections can help us get gigs. Her sister was president of the high-school social club last year. They have formals and crush parties all the time, and they hire bands."

The social club and gigs comment wasn't an entirely lousy idea. Haley could help them get gigs if they ever got good enough to play in public. Gigs would be cool—exposure, money . . . "We'll give her a shot," Tig said. "A shot. Not a guarantee. If she stinks, she's out. No remorse."

"It's going to be great!" Kyra said. "You, me, and Haley are in a band!"

"We're not 'in a band,' " said Tig. "We're two girls just beginning music lessons and another who might be able to sing—*might*. We need some actual musicians on board before we can call ourselves a band. As of right now we still don't have a band."

Chapter Six

"So, you have a band now?" Will asked at lunch.

"Word gets around fast," Tig replied, glaring at Kyra.

"Need a drummer?"

"No," Tig said.

They were interrupted by Kyra's shouting. "Haley! Over here!" Haley, who was standing in the lunch line with Regan, looked at Kyra as though she had leprosy, and then turned her back to her. Undaunted, Kyra announced to the rest of the table, "Maybe another time."

Will kept on. "Who've you got for your drummer? Anybody I know?"

Tig pretended to be absorbed in carefully opening her pack of cookies.

"I said, who's your drummer?" Will repeated.

"I don't want to talk about it," Tig said.

"Why not? Everybody already knows Haley's fronting your band. So what's your job? You play piano or something? Like doing the keyboard?"

The keyboard.

"Olivia, you play piano, right?" Tig asked.

"Yeah, sorta," Olivia said. "I mean, I took lessons for, like, forever, when I was little. My mom finally let me quit last year when I got so busy with tennis." Olivia was constantly in the local paper for winning yet another tennis tournament, and everyone assumed she'd go to UA or somewhere on a full tennis scholarship one day.

"You want to be in our band?" Tig asked. "Play the keyboard?"

Olivia raised her eyebrows, intrigued. "Sounds

fun," she said, "but I haven't played in a long time. My piano is covered with dust."

"But could you get an electronic keyboard?"

"I actually have one at my aunt's house," Olivia said. "I'm sure I could bring it home. But really, I don't know how to play anything cool."

"But you can read music. You could play something cool if you had the sheet music?"

"Yeah, sure."

"So join our band. It'll be fun."

"I don't know," Olivia said. "I have tennis practice and tournaments, and—"

"We can work around that," Tig said. "I promise. We won't interfere with your tennis at all. Just say yes!"

Olivia smiled. "Okay, then. I guess so!"

"I want to be in the band," Will said. "You need a drummer, don't you?"

"No, we don't," Tig replied.

"So you do have a drummer," Will said. "Who is it?"

"None of your business."

"Why all the secrecy?" Will asked. "You never told

me what you're playing. Or are you the singer?"

Tig picked at her sandwich.

"Wait a minute," Will said. "You're the drummer, aren't you?"

Tig didn't look up.

"That's it! You're the drummer!"

"Fine," Tig said. "Go ahead. Have your fun. Get it out of your system."

Will grinned. "I'm not going to make fun of you. I think it's . . . cute."

Tig cut her eyes at him. "Yeah, that's what I'm going for. Cute."

"So, do you play? Where'd you learn? You have a drum set?"

"I got a decent set," Tig said. "And I've had a few lessons." Tig didn't want Will to know she'd been taking lessons for nearly two months—he might expect her to be a lot better than she was. "So I can't really play well yet, but I'm working on it."

"That's cool," Will said. "Show me something." He handed her the sticks from his back pocket.

Tentatively, Tig took them.

On the lunch-room table, she did a quick flam, followed by a couple of fills, using Olivia's and Kyra's fabric lunch bags as toms.

Tig could feel her face getting red as Will grinned at her. "You're laughing at me," she said.

"No, I'm not," Will said. "That wasn't bad. But drums are both arms *and* legs. I didn't see any movement here." He put his hand on her left knee — then quickly removed it.

"I don't know what to do with the hi-hat leg yet," Tig said. "But my teacher says I've got to work on really pounding the kick. I'm practicing hitting the bass hard enough that I get the right reverberation."

"Yeah, you've got to really put your thigh into it, especially at first," Will said. "The ankle alone just doesn't deliver the power. So, have you ever tried holding the left stick underhanded, like this?"

Will and Tig discussed the pros and cons of overhand versus underhand left stick and tilted versus untilted toms until the bell rang.

As they packed up, Will said, "We should play together sometime." Then Will blushed. "That sounded weird. I don't mean, like, G.I. Joes. Not that I still play G.I. Joes or anything, but . . . you know what I mean."

Tig nodded. She knew what he meant. Or at least, she thought she did.

Chapter Seven

After a few months of weekly lessons with Lee, Tig now had some idea of what she was doing on the drums; it wasn't just *crash, crash, clang,* like a four-year-old randomly hitting things. There was actual rhythm. She'd learned that most rock songs had the basic boom-chick or boom-boom-chick pattern, and now she could easily tell the booms from the chicks. Using an app to slow down the tempo, she was able to follow along with her phone on a few songs, at least until they got to the bridge.

Lee had her practicing a basic four-count with the

bass on two before the snare. She'd finally gotten to the point where she could stay on count. When she'd first started, she'd get so excited about getting the pattern right, she'd speed up.

"Good," Lee said when she'd demonstrated mastery of the pattern. "Keep going, just like that."

While Tig kept banging out the pattern, Lee went to his electronic keyboard and began playing. Tig kept on as he played along. "Recognize that?" he asked.

Tig stopped. "Is that 'Sweet Home Alabama'?"

"Yes, ma'am," Lee replied.

Tig grinned. "You mean I just played part of 'Sweet Home Alabama'? That's the pattern you've had me working on all these weeks? I didn't even know that's what I was doing!"

"It's different when you put the other instruments with it," he said. "I just wanted to give you a little sense of what it's like to play with other musicians."

Tig told him about how she'd been knocking out drumbeats to songs on her phone.

"That's good," Lee said. "It's like playing with a real

band. Great idea. Just make sure you practice with a metronome. Remember, the drummer's got to keep the pace."

When Tig got home, she called Kyra. "How's the bass coming?"

"It's okay," Kyra said. "I can do a few things on it."

"Good," Tig replied. "Keep practicing. Tell your teacher you want to learn 'Sweet Home Alabama.'"

"Why?"

"Because I can play most of it on my drums," Tig said. "It will be our first song."

"Why'd you pick that one?"

"I didn't, exactly. Lee did. He taught me to play it before I knew what it was. But it's a good choice. A crowd-pleaser. They play it on the loudspeaker at the football games; it's like the town song, you know?"

"Okay," Kyra said. "Wow, won't it be neat to be able to play a real song together? You think Olivia can do it?"

"Olivia reads music. She can handle it." Tig thought a moment. "We've got to get a guitar player."

"Tell Will to learn the guitar," Kyra said. "He's

dying to be in our band."

"He doesn't know it's all girls," Tig said.

"He doesn't care. He just knows you're in it."

"What's that supposed to mean?"

"Duh!" Kyra said. "He's totally crushing on you!"

"What-ever! He is not."

"Come on—you know he is. Don't you think he's kind of cute?"

"Um, *no*. No, I do not. Besides, he doesn't play guitar, and even if he did, it's going to be an all-girl band. Now get serious. Who do we know who plays the guitar?"

"I can't think of anyone," Kyra said. "At least not a girl."

There had to be a girl at Lakeview Heights who played the guitar. *Think, Tig, think*, she told herself.

"I've got it," Tig said.

"Who?" Kyra asked.

"You're not going to like it."

Chapter Eight

Kyra was against it from the first mention. Robbie Chan was on the completely opposite end of the social spectrum from Haley Thornton. All that Kyra had hoped to accomplish by inviting Haley into the band would be undone by inviting Robbie.

Which was yet another reason why Tig thought it was a fantastic plan.

Robbie Chan wasn't exactly beautiful, but she was so interesting-looking, only careful analysis would reveal that. This, along with her surly attitude, was probably why the popular clique wanted absolutely nothing to do with her. She'd gotten her shiny, stick-straight hair from her dad, and her quirky sense of style from her New York City–native mother. Robbie Chan was entirely too cool for Lakeview Heights. Except for the fact that her parents were university professors, she wouldn't have been in Tuscaloosa, Alabama, at all. She didn't fit in at school even in the slightest, and she seemed just fine with that. She usually sat in the back unless there was a seating chart, and she hung with the weirdos. She wore a thick purple streak in her long hair and generally had a couple of leather bracelets on her wrists. But what had caught Tig's attention lately was her necklace with the silver guitar pendant.

Okay, maybe the guitar pendant was just for looks. It didn't mean she actually played.

But at least it was a conversation starter.

Students sat in the gym before the first bell each morning, and specific sections had been claimed by specific groups. There was the genius area with the academic overachievers, the jock area with the athletes, and of course, the Bot Spot, where the popular girls held court. Tig left the safety of her section of the gym, which was populated with the regular kids who didn't really identify anywhere else, and climbed to the top of the bleachers, where the social outcasts sat. Robbie wasn't talking to anyone, just zoning out with whatever tune was playing through her earbuds.

"S'up?" Tig asked, sitting on the bleacher in front of Robbie.

Robbie just kind of looked at her, almost as though she weren't sure Tig had actually addressed her.

Tig tried again. "How's it going?"

Robbie grimaced and pulled out her left earbud. "Fine?" Her reply seemed to come with an unspoken *What do you want?*

"What're you listening to?" Tig asked.

Now Robbie pulled the earbud out of her right ear and asked, with definite annoyance, "What?"

"I said, what are you listening to?"

"Music," Robbie said.

"Duh," said Tig. "Thanks for clearing that up." Tig

tried to make it sound like a joke but was worried it sounded mean.

"Did you want something?" Robbie asked.

"I was just making conversation," Tig said.

"Why?"

"Because I'm a nice person?"

Robbie rolled her eyes and put the bud back into her ear.

"Okay, look," Tig said. Robbie took the bud out once again and sighed. Tig continued. "Your necklace. I wanted to ask you about it."

"I got it online. I forget where."

"Do you play the guitar?"

"Why do you want to know?"

"Do you or not? It's a simple question, not the Spanish Inquisition."

"Yeah, a little," Robbie said. "I started lessons in fourth grade, when I finally convinced my mom to let me switch from cello. Why?"

"A few of us are starting up a band. All girls. Going to be really cool. We need a guitar player. Thought you might be up for it."

"Are you guys any good?" Robbie was probably the only person in school who would say *you guys* instead of *y'all*. Tig sort of liked it.

"Truthfully? No." Tig laughed.

"Well, at least you're honest," said Robbie. She almost smiled. "Who's in the band, and what are your skills?"

"I'm the drummer," Tig said. "I'm just learning, but I can handle a basic boom-chick, and I'm taking lessons once a week. My cousin Kyra's on bass. She's right about where I am. Olivia's going to do the keyboard."

"Olivia the tennis girl?"

"Yeah. She took piano when she was little, so she can read music and pretty much do whatever."

"Okay," Robbie said. "She's nice. But which one of you sings? Because I don't sing."

"Oh, me neither," said Tig. "Actually, we have a singer, kind of. It's really on a trial basis. Kyra recruited her, sort of without consulting me, and—"

"Who?"

Tig took a deep breath. "Haley Thornton."

Robbie raised her hands and leaned back. "No way! Not happening!"

"That's exactly what I said!" Tig replied. "But Kyra had already asked her. And I don't know how to get out of it. I promised Kyra I'd let Haley have a shot, but I'm not committed to anything."

"I am *so* not hanging with a Bot," Robbie said.

"That's what I said! I even called her a Bot!" Tig leaned in. "This is why I need you, Robbie. You get it. Listen, I don't have any skills to speak of. I'm really green. Maybe you're a novice on the guitar; maybe you're great.... I don't know. But you *get* it, you know? You're so . . . You're so rock 'n' roll."

Robbie's expression softened. She seemed to like the description.

Tig continued. "Come on, please? Give us a try. I bet you and I will get along great. And Olivia and Kyra are really nice. Besides, you can't leave me to deal with Haley Thornton on my own, right?"

"Maybe I could. I'm not big on riding in to the

rescue."

"What if I told you that several weeks ago Will Mason told me, and I quote, 'Girl bands are gimmicks.' And girl bands never work 'because girls can't get along.'"

"Oh, no, he didn't!" Robbie said.

"He did," Tig replied. "I've got to prove him wrong."

Robbie smiled. "Okay, Antigone," she said. "I'll do it."

"Okay, Roberta."

Robbie shook her head. "The first day of school roll call is a double-edged sword. I guess if we're going to be in a band together, we can go by Tig and Robbie."

"Those names are very rock 'n' roll, don't you think?"

"Um, *yeah!*"

"Awesome," Tig said.

"By the way, what's the name of our band?" Robbie asked.

A name hadn't even occurred to Tig yet. "Let me get back to you on that," she said.

Chapter Nine

Tig spent the night at Kyra's that Friday. Tig's mom and dad had taken her younger sibs on a youth retreat for the elementary grades, and Tig had told them she'd rather spend the weekend in a fire ant bed. She'd assumed she'd be dumped with her grandparents to chill out all weekend while her grandmother brought her snacks every five minutes, but they, too, were going out of town. They'd invited her to come along to her grandmother's nursing school reunion, but Tig didn't want to be oohed and aahed over by little old ladies all weekend, so it was Kyra's or nothing. Not that she minded hanging with Kyra and Uncle Nick, of course. But half a weekend with Aunt Laurie almost made a fire ant bed sound appealing.

"Don't stay up too late, you two," Aunt Laurie had said after dinner while Tig and Kyra were cleaning up the dishes. "We have the charity walk tomorrow bright and early. Antigone, you did bring something suitable to wear, didn't you?"

"Oh, sure," Tig replied. "My evening gown is in my duffel bag."

Aunt Laurie fake laughed. "Seriously, though."

"Yes, ma'am," Tig said. She'd packed a pair of the running shorts all the girls wore, and her tennis shoes were a socially acceptable brand. "Don't worry. I'll try not to embarrass you."

"Don't be silly, Antigone," Aunt Laurie said without a hint of sincerity.

Tig was certain that Aunt Laurie didn't want her anywhere near the charity run. Events like this were Aunt Laurie's opportunity to hobnob with the influential folk, and better yet, to have Kyra hobnob with their daughters. Not that Kyra seemed to mind much. Hobnobbing was not a priority Tig had picked up from her mother, who couldn't care less about such things, and therefore was not a skill set Tig had ever mastered.

"I have T-shirts for you both," Aunt Laurie said. "All the participants will be wearing them."

Uncle Nick laughed. "Does anything happen in this town without somebody printing a T-shirt about it?"

"I know, right?" Tig said. "It's, like, if a tree falls in a forest and no one is around to hear it, does it make a sound? And if something happens in Tuscaloosa and no one makes a T-shirt for it, did it really even happen?"

Uncle Nick laughed. "Hey, here's one from when I was at UA: How many frat guys does it take to screw in a lightbulb?"

Tig thought. "I don't know. How many?"

"Three. One to screw in the lightbulb and the other two to order the T-shirts."

Tig and Uncle Nick laughed, but Aunt Laurie frowned. "This event raises money for charity," she said. "We are helping the less fortunate."

Uncle Nick cleared his throat. "Of course you are," he said, and kissed Aunt Laurie's cheek. But when she wasn't looking, he winked at Tig, who grinned back at him. It wasn't that Tig was against charity events in general; she knew some of the moms in these clubs cared deeply about helping others and wanted to do something positive for the town. It was just that she also knew Aunt Laurie wasn't one of those women.

"What color is the T-shirt?" Kyra asked.

"Beige," Aunt Laurie said. "Hideous. I tried to get them to do blue, but no one would listen. I know the girls usually walk together, but try to run at least a little bit to keep some color in your cheeks so the beige doesn't completely wash you out."

The next morning at the park, the minute after they pinned their race numbers to the backs of their shirts, Kyra went on Bot Patrol.

"Do you see Haley, Regan, and Sofia?" she asked Tig.

"No, and I've been looking *everywhere!*" Tig replied sarcastically.

The sarcasm was lost on Kyra, who responded, "I think I see them over there! Come on!" and then dragged Tig by her hideous beige T-shirt right toward them.

"Hey, chicas!" Kyra said. Tig was embarrassed for her. The Bots barely even looked at them, but Kyra kept pressing. "Ready to run?"

"Nobody's running," Regan said. "I'm not going to sweat like a pig for some stupid race. Like I care if this town has universal pre-K." All three of them had matching ponytail holders, and their T-shirts were tied in a small knot on their right hips. Their running shorts were all gray with pink trim, and their running shoes were all the same brand. Tig noticed Kyra was tying her T-shirt into a knot on her right hip, too.

An announcer told everyone to line up for the race. Kyra kept herself glued to the three popular girls, but Tig hung back. Soon she was lost in the runners and walkers and could no longer see Kyra or the other girls at all. As the race began, Tig fell into an easy pace of fast walking. The sound of her feet against the pavement created a nice rhythm. She hadn't noticed that she'd quickly caught up with Kyra and the Bots. "There you are!" Kyra said, grabbing Tig's arm and slowing her pace. "I was just saying to Regan that it's so cool that Haley's singing in our band. Right, Regan?"

"If you say so," Regan replied.

"Regan, is your mom going to work the golf tournament next month?" Kyra asked. "My mom said she hopes she will. My mom's in charge of the raffle."

"I don't know," Regan said, not even looking at Kyra.

"Haley, we can save a seat for you Monday at lunch—and Regan . . . Really, we have room for all of you—if you want to talk about song selection for the band and stuff," Kyra said. "Or, you know, we could come sit with you, if that'd be better."

Tig blushed. She saw Haley make a face at Regan, and Regan rolled her eyes.

"Look, I said I'd sing in your little band, not take

you on as a project," Haley said.

Kyra laughed. Laughed!

Get a backbone, Tig thought. "Nobody needs you to take on any projects. Really," Tig said.

Regan cut in. "Good thing," Regan said. "Because all Haley's singing in your band means is that Haley likes to sing. Not that y'all are suddenly besties."

"I'm glad we understand one another," Tig said. "And guess what else? It suits me just fine if Haley doesn't want to sing with us. We don't need her."

"Haley wants to sing with us!" Kyra said. "Don't you, Haley?"

Haley looked at Regan. "I do love to sing," she said, as though asking Regan's permission.

"Then sing," Regan said. "Oh, look. My shoe is suddenly untied. Hales, Sof, come help me tie it." The three of them cut through the other runners to the sidewalk. Kyra was about to follow them, but this time Tig grabbed Kyra's arm and made her continue walking.

"How can you let them treat you that way?" Tig

demanded. "You're better than that! You're Kyra Bennett! And Bennett girls don't take anybody's attitude!"

"Don't be so sensitive," Kyra said. "Mama said that Regan's mom said that Regan told her she really likes me. Mama said I just need to make more of an effort."

"Yeah, well, your mom doesn't seem to mind if that effort blows up in your face," Tig said. "They're not nice girls, Kyra. They're just not."

"We only need to get to know them better," Kyra replied. "The band will help us do that."

Tig couldn't think of another thing to say. So, in her best Southern belle voice, she cried, "Oh my! This beige T-shirt is washing out my skin tone! I must run and get some color in my cheeks!"

Tig looked back only once but saw that Kyra was again making her way toward the Bots.

Chapter Ten

In news that shocked no one but Kyra, the Bots did not sit with them Monday at lunch. Or Tuesday. Or ever. This suited Tig just fine but confused Kyra, who'd thought she'd done so well at Saturday's run.

The band's first practice was set for Tuesday after school. Tig had told the other girls to work on "Sweet Home Alabama."

They met at the green house at four p.m. Haley was the last to arrive. Her mother didn't so much as wave as she pulled away; she was too busy scrunching her face into a look of disdain as she turned around on the gravel driveway. "I have to be done by the time my mom's manicure is over," Haley said.

Robbie shot a look at Tig. Kyra said, "I'm sure that will be plenty of time. Ooh, I love your blush!" Kyra herded Haley into the house.

"I've got a bad feeling about this," Robbie said to Tig and Olivia.

"That makes two of us," Tig replied.

Once everything was set up—amps plugged in, Haley's microphone hot, all that stuff—Tig suggested a run-through first on the instruments, no vocals. Haley protested until she could see that Tig wouldn't give in to her.

"Whatevs," Haley finally said.

Tig counted off on her sticks, and Robbie began playing the guitar intro. As soon as Tig and Kyra joined in, it occurred to Tig that the two of them should probably have practiced together before everyone else showed up. They had to start over a few times to get the beat right, playing at an embarrassingly slow count for an embarrassingly long time. Tig found that her coordination was shot with that many people watching and waiting on her. Eventually she got it right, but not without saying, "Wait, let me try that again," about fifty times.

Robbie and Olivia were both good. Tig felt embarrassed that she and Kyra were so obviously light-years behind them in skill level.

"I'm sorry, y'all," Tig said. "Kyra and I are pretty green."

"Everybody's green at first," Robbie said. "It's all good. We'll get there."

"Can I sing now?" Haley asked with obvious frustration.

"Yeah, sure," Tig replied. "Let's take it from the top, this time with vocals."

They somehow managed to start the song at almost the right rhythm, and Haley began singing the first verse.

Tig looked at Robbie, then at Olivia. They were both grimacing. Tig looked next at Kyra, who smiled and shrugged. It wasn't just that Haley was off-key much of the time. It was that everything about her singing was wrong.

Tig waited until the end of the song. "So, Haley . . . ," she began.

"You're welcome," Haley said.

Tig fake laughed to be polite. "Yeah, that was . . . You really, um . . . enunciated."

"That's what they teach you to do in professional singing classes," Haley said. "Crisp diction. And, of course, volume, so that the back of the theater can hear you."

"Or, you know, you could kind of let the microphone help with that," Robbie said.

"Yeah, maybe Robbie's got a point. You might want to take it down a notch on the volume, and since this is sort of a Southern anthem, maybe loosen up the diction a little bit. Give it some flavor, know what I mean?"

Haley scrunched up her face. "You want me to sing badly to match your drumming?"

Before Tig could launch into Haley, Kyra interrupted. "Ha, ha, ha! Good one, Haley! Oh, don't you love this girl-band banter?"

"Let's take it from the top again," Haley suggested.

"Yes, let's do that," Tig agreed, neglecting to add, *Even though it's my band, and I'm the one who says when we take it from the top. But whatever.*

They ran through the song three more times, each time with the same result as the first, before Haley's mom drove up. "Later," Haley said. "And maybe you could practice on your own before next week. You know, to try not to stink quite so much."

Kyra waved as Haley jumped into the car and it pulled away. Robbie, Olivia, and Tig just stared in a sort of daze. Had Haley really just said that? And had practice really been as bad as they thought?

Robbie broke the silence. "You do realize you're going to have to do something about that?"

"Yeah," Tig said. "Definitely."

Chapter Eleven

By the next practice, Tig and Kyra were better on their instruments. Kyra had spent the weekend at Tig's, and they'd practiced together nonstop. Tig was becoming enough of a musician to realize that the bass and the drums walked hand in hand, and that together they were the foundation of the band's sound. A little scary considering that they were the two least experienced members of the group, but Robbie's guitar and Olivia's keyboard were held up by what Tig and Kyra put down.

Each musician was improving separately, which

made the band sound a little better together.

Except for Haley. And not just in the area of musicianship. Haley was becoming harder to take every time Tig was around her.

"What's the name of this band?" Haley demanded at the third practice.

"Good question," Tig said. It was something she'd wanted to address with the girls; she just hadn't planned on doing it on Haley's timetable. Still, she tried to be diplomatic: no sense in becoming a Bot target if she could avoid it. "Does anyone have any suggestions?"

"I've got one," Robbie said. "How about Blood Lust?"

"Ewww," Olivia said.

"Ewww what?" Robbie asked. "The blood or the lust?"

"Both," Olivia said. "I'm squeamish. And my mom would *freak* if I told her I was in a band with *lust* in the name. She does *not* approve of lust."

"Okay," Robbie said. "You got a better idea, then?"

"I was thinking, something cute and fun," Olivia

said. "How about the Kittens?"

Robbie laughed. "Did you run that one past your mom?"

"No. Why?"

"The term *kitten* is a provocative way to describe females," Robbie explained. "I doubt your mom would like it. And I'd be right there with her. I refuse to be part of anything that objectifies women and girls."

"Ewww," Olivia repeated. "I didn't know. So, that's definitely out. Anybody got something better?"

"What about something concepty . . . simple . . . like, the Five?" Kyra said.

"Two words," Haley said. *"Bore. Ring."*

Although Tig kind of agreed with Haley, she didn't like the way she'd dismissed Kyra so rudely. "And what do you suggest, Haley?" she asked.

"Call it what it is: Haley and the Other Girls," Haley said.

"You're not serious," Robbie replied.

"Of course I'm serious," said Haley.

"Why stop there?" Tig said. "Why not just call our

band Haley and the Sycophants?"

Robbie laughed. "While I actually find that ironic and attention-getting, and I do love the way the word *sycophant* rolls off the tongue, I will agree to that when it snows in Alabama in August."

"What's a sycophant?" Haley asked.

"Forget it," Tig said. She looked down at her mythology book sitting on top of her backpack in the corner. Another decision Tig needed to make was which myth from English class to write her essay about. Now she was ready to make two decisions at once. "I've got it," she said. "How about Pandora's Box?"

"I like it," Robbie said. "Cool. Dangerous. So cool it makes me wonder why I've never heard of a band using it before. Did you do an Internet search?"

"Not yet," Tig said. She grabbed her phone and typed in the search terms. "It says there was a female band in the '80s who called themselves Pandora's Box, but they only had one album and it didn't get much attention."

"Never heard of them," said Robbie. Neither had anyone else.

"I'll ask an expert." Tig texted both her parents, who replied almost immediately. "My mom and my dad both say it doesn't ring a bell, and those two know '80s music like nobody's business. If they don't know who they are, probably no one else does, either."

Robbie, Kyra, and Olivia also texted their parents, who also had never heard of the band.

"Just so long as we're not derivative," Robbie said. "I say we snag it!"

"Pandora's Box? What does it mean?" Haley asked.

"You know, the myth," Tig said. "It's this box full of all the trouble in the world, and they aren't supposed to open it, but when they do, whammo!"

"That's stupid," Haley said. "Just close the box. Problem solved."

Tig and Robbie looked at each other and shook their heads.

"I like it," Olivia said. "What about you, Kyra?"

Kyra looked at Haley. Tig could tell she didn't want

to cross her. "I guess we should pick something we all like," Kyra said.

"Simple question," Robbie said. "Do you, Kyra, like the name Pandora's Box?"

"I mean," Kyra said, "I do, but—"

"Then it looks like it's four to one," Robbie said. "Don't you just love democracy?"

"But I don't like that name," Haley said.

"Maybe we should just get back to practicing," Tig said. "We can all let the name sink in for a little while. You might like it better after you sleep on it."

"No, I won't," Haley said. But Tig just counted off for the next run-through of "Sweet Home Alabama" to end the conversation, and everyone started playing.

In the middle of the song, though, Haley stopped singing and barked out an order. "Write this down," she said to Tig.

"Excuse me?" Tig replied.

"Hurry . . . grab some paper before I lose my train of thought."

"What are you—" But before Tig could finish,

Haley interrupted again.

"Paper!" She actually snapped her fingers.

Tig was too taken aback to know exactly how to respond, but Kyra quickly pulled a notebook from her backpack. "I've got it," Kyra said. "Go ahead."

"Octave change after the bridge, and slow it down on the chorus."

As Kyra wrote, Tig said, "No. Absolutely not."

"I beg your pardon?" Haley said.

"No octave change. No slowing down the chorus."

"But that's the way I want to sing it," Haley said.

"But that's not the way we want to play it," Tig replied. She looked at the rest of the band. "Am I right?"

Olivia and Kyra looked like frightened deer and said nothing.

"You're right," Robbie said.

"Last time I checked, I'm the lead singer," Haley said.

"Last time I checked, this was Tig's band," Robbie shot back.

"Says who?" Haley asked.

"Says all of us," Robbie said. "Or in case you hadn't noticed, this is Tig's rehearsal space, and the band was her idea."

"Look, it doesn't really matter who's the leader and who's the singer," Tig added, thinking, *Of course it matters*. But being brought up in the Deep South, Tig had been trained to believe that good manners were the only thing that kept society from complete collapse. Manners, Tig had been taught, were the grease that turned the wheels of the social machine, and they were the duty of every Southern girl. Her mother had taught her that being nice, even when she didn't feel like it, wasn't being fake, as Tig had supposed; instead it was being "gracious." Tig wanted to be gracious and lovely like her mother and grand-mothers, but she wondered how they managed it when people like Haley were so downright awful. "The point is what makes the song work best for our group," Tig continued. "And slowing down the chorus makes it drag too much. Remember, this is a crowd favorite. They're going to want to hear it played the way they know it."

"That's only because they haven't heard me sing it better," Haley said.

"Are you actually suggesting that you sing this better than—" Robbie was cut off by a horn honking outside.

Kyra looked out the window and said, "That's your mom, Haley."

"Good," Haley replied. "You'll have time to think about it when I'm gone. And I suggest you think about it long and hard. I'm the only thing this pathetic excuse for a band has going for it."

Kyra actually said, "Bye, Haley!" as Haley stormed out of the studio. Well, it was the same old concrete house, but the girls had taken to referring to it as "the studio."

"She's got to go," Robbie said.

"She is pretty horrible," Olivia added.

"Tig, no!" Kyra said. "Give her a chance!"

"For Pete's sake, Kyra, we've given her a chance!

More than one!" said Tig. "Even Olivia thinks she's horrible, and Olivia's nicer than . . . than Winnie-the-Pooh!"

Everyone cracked up. "Winnie-the-Pooh," Robbie repeated. "Nice."

"I'm spent," Olivia said. "I can't think about this anymore today. I've got to work on my mythology essay for English."

"Me too," said Robbie.

"Look," said Tig, "what's say we get together this weekend and have some downtime as a band? A band retreat, if you will. Slumber party at my house Friday night? Complete with stupid movies and lots of snacks. What do y'all say?"

"I'm in," said Robbie. Olivia and Kyra said they were too, if it was okay with their moms, but Olivia would have to leave early Saturday to make a tennis lesson.

"I'll invite Haley tomorrow," Kyra volunteered.

"Who said anything about Haley?" Robbie said.

"Well, she's in the band," said Kyra. "I can invite

her, can't I, Tig?"

Tig sighed. She was tired of fighting and didn't want to get into it with Kyra at the moment. "I suppose so." She suspected—and hoped—that Haley would refuse the invitation.

"I just remembered I've got a home improvement project this weekend," Robbie said.

"Oh, no, you don't," Tig said. "We're in this together. Hey, thanks for having my back—you know, with the chorus and octave thing."

"No problem."

"Band party at Tig's Friday night," Olivia said as she typed a note into her phone. "It might be fun."

Tig knew what Olivia was thinking. *It might be fun . . . if Haley doesn't show up.*

Chapter Twelve

"The more I think about the name Pandora's Box, the more I like it for our band," Robbie told Tig the next day at lunch. Robbie had taken to sitting at what had now become the band's table. Well, minus Haley, of course, and plus Will and Sam, who took the edge seats next to the guys' table.

"Your band's name is Pandora's Box?" Will asked. "I dig that."

Tig didn't respond. She felt embarrassed but couldn't say why. She just did. Lately everything Will said or did made her feel . . . What was it she felt? Tig wasn't sure. But every time Will was around, she felt it.

"So, how's Haley working out?" Will said.

Tig looked at Olivia, Kyra, and Robbie. No one said a word.

"I take it that means not so good," said Will. "What? She can't sing?"

"Of course she can sing," Robbie said. "Haley's the best singer ever. Just ask Haley!"

Tig grinned. "She's all right."

"No, Tig," Robbie said. "What you mean is, she's all riiiiii—iiii—iii—iiight!" Robbie pulled her hand down in a fist while singing the word in twenty different notes and about ten syllables.

Will laughed. "No way! She's a warbler?"

"Is Haley a warbler?" Robbie laughed. "Was John Locke an influential thinker during the Enlightenment?" Robbie laughed some more, but everyone else just stared at her. Robbie stopped laughing. "The answer is yes. Yes, he was. Man, don't you people know your basic historical references? Sheesh."

"Haley's a bit of a diva," Olivia said. "Except that

she can't really sing."

"Olivia!" said Kyra.

"Well, she can't," Olivia said. "I mean, I'm just sayin'."

"Aww, man," said Will. "There goes your edge. You can't have a pop-soul diva front a rock band. Especially one who can't really even sing."

"Did you hear that, Kyra?" Tig asked.

"Oh, so now we're listening to Will all of a sudden?" said Kyra.

"What are you going to do?" Will said. "Give her the old heave-ho?"

"I don't know," Tig said. "I've got to do something, but I'm not looking forward to the confrontation."

"Oh, *I'm* looking forward to the confrontation!" Robbie said. "Can I have the confrontation? Please? I would savor it. Let me kick her out. I'll totally do it."

"Give her one more chance," Kyra said. "Please? Everyone will think we're mean if we kick her out now."

"Everyone who? Regan and Sofia? Who cares?" Robbie said. "I'm not scared of them."

"Me neither," Tig said. But deep down, she was a little bit scared. What drama would result in kicking Haley out of the band? Regan and Haley and Sofia may have been annoying Bots, but Tig had a feeling they knew how to bring it when crossed. Running the school social hierarchy wasn't the kind of thing that happened by accident.

"One more practice," Kyra said. "Please, Tig."

Tig sighed. "Okay. One. But that's it. We'll see how it goes. We'll practice Friday after school, before the sleepover. Then we'll discuss."

"Can I come?" Will asked.

"To the practice?" said Tig.

"Or the sleepover. I'm not picky."

Tig elbowed him. "In your dreams." She didn't want Will anywhere near practice. She didn't need him critiquing her drumming. She was still too green.

"I'll go ask Haley if Friday works for her," Kyra said. Everyone stared at her. "What? You already said I could invite her to the sleepover! And she needs to be at practice." Before anyone could say anything else,

Kyra was on her way to Haley and Regan's table.

Tig, Olivia, Robbie, and Will watched from across the lunch room. Kyra's posture showed her nervousness, and the smile plastered on her face was forced. Regan looked at her with revulsion, and Haley barely looked at her at all. Haley waved her hand in dismissal, and Kyra returned to Tig's table.

"She said she'll think about it," Kyra said.

"Did you hear that, Tig?" Robbie asked. "Haley's going to think about it! Oh, joy! Oh, happy day! To think that peasants such as ourselves should be so honored!"

"What's so bad about thinking about it?" Kyra said.

"Nothing," Tig replied. "Let's just see how it goes on Friday."

Chapter Thirteen

Tig didn't think it was possible for Haley to be more obnoxious, but on Friday she outdid herself.

When she got to practice, she announced, "You've got thirty minutes of my time. Make it count. It's Friday, and I have plans."

"You're not staying for the sleepover?" Kyra asked.

Haley laughed. "Did you miss the part where I said I have plans?"

When they began practicing, Haley was all over the map. First there was the tempo issue. Even though the rest of the band had told her at the last practice that they wouldn't slow down the song, Haley sang it the way she wanted to. She dragged and put in vocal flourishes as she saw fit, paying no attention to what the other band members were doing.

"Haley, part of being in a band is listening to the other members," Tig said. "If we all just do our own thing, we're not a band. We're just a bunch of people making noise in the same general area."

"Does the term *lead* singer mean anything to you people?" Haley asked. "Lead. As in, get your act together and start following me."

"Listen, Haley . . . ," Tig began.

"From the top," Haley said. Then she counted off and cranked the song through her phone, which she'd hooked up to a speaker. Tig couldn't believe she'd actually counted off! And Kyra fell in on bass with the recording. Tig, once again too shocked to think straight, fell in behind Kyra, and Olivia started in on the keyboard.

Then Robbie jumped in.

But what Robbie played was nothing at all like

"Sweet Home Alabama." Her guitar was squealing and whining all over the place, her hand running up and down the frets at a speed none of her bandmates could've matched, even if they had known what in the world she was playing.

Haley clicked off her phone, put her hands over her ears, and shouted, "What are you doing?"

Robbie played a couple more licks before stopping. "Oh, I'm sorry. Was I supposed to wait for the rest of you? Were we supposed to be playing something together? I mean, I am *lead* guitar, so I figured you'd all just, you know, follow me. Or wait . . . was that completely self-centered?"

Tig couldn't help but smirk. "Okay, Robbie. You've made your point."

"Have I?" Robbie asked. "Haley, do you think I've made my point?"

"Here's *my* point," Haley said. "My mom's going to be here any minute. And then I'm out of here because I have more important things to do than hang around with a bunch of people who don't appreciate what I have to offer. While you're having your little sleepover, you can work out how you're going to deal with this. Because frankly, Robbie, I don't like your attitude. So you have a choice: either fix it or find another band."

Tig had had it. "Wait just a minute! You don't get to go around kicking people out of *my* band!"

"Don't kid yourself," Haley said. "This may have been your idea, and this may be your pitiful little building to rehearse in, but make no mistake: this is *my* band. The only reason we'd ever get booked would be because of me. The only reason anyone would come hear us play is because of me. In short, this band is nothing without me. You don't even *exist* without me. So you either fix her or get rid of her. And those are my final words."

They heard a car pull up in the gravel and the horn honk. "Later," Haley said.

The other girls watched in silence as her car pulled away.

Finally Tig said, "There are no words. Just . . . no words."

"You wouldn't really kick me out of the band, would you?" Robbie asked.

Tig started laughing. Olivia did too. Even Kyra couldn't help but join in.

"Well, at least somebody likes me," said Robbie. "And to think, after I tried so hard to be nice to her!"

"This is all my fault," Kyra said.

No one said anything.

"Isn't anyone going to disagree with me?" Kyra asked. "Someone's supposed to say, 'No, Kyra, it's not your fault.'"

Tig shrugged, and even Kyra sort of laughed before continuing. "Okay, okay, it's my fault. Look, I know she's got to go, but what do you think she'll do if we kick her out? And where are we going to find another lead singer?"

"I'm worn-out," Olivia said. "I'm too tired and too hungry to process this. Let's go grab some supper, and then we can obsess."

It was agreed. They wouldn't think about the Haley problem until after dinner.

Tig couldn't help but worry, though. It was her band, and she'd be the one who'd have to get rid of Haley. Why did Kyra have to get her into this mess? There was no telling what Haley, along with Regan and Sofia, might do to get back at her. Plus, if the band failed once Haley was out, the Bots would tell everyone it was because Pandora's Box couldn't make it without Haley.

Tig couldn't let that happen. She'd have to find a lead singer who would bring something special to the band, somebody who could front like nobody's business, somebody with a special something that would bring in an audience and attract a following.

If she was going to kick Haley out, she'd have to replace her with someone amazing.

But where in Tuscaloosa, Alabama, in her realm of middle-school girls, was she supposed to find this person?

Chapter Fourteen

At Pepe's Grill, Tig's mom and dad sat with her sibs at a separate table in the back so Tig wouldn't have to be seen with them, which Tig thought was pretty decent on their part. Robbie, Olivia, Kyra, and Tig sat in a booth next to a raised platform made out of plywood. There was a microphone on a stand and a screen in front of it.

While the waiter took their drink orders, Tig asked, "What gives with the little stage?"

"You didn't see the sign?" the waiter asked.

"What sign?"

"Karaoke Fridays! You going to sing for us?"

Tig laughed. "I don't sing."

"That's what makes it fun," he said.

"Ooh! We could do a duet!" Kyra said. "Want to see what songs they have?"

"I'll pass," Tig said. "But, Olivia, feel free."

Olivia smiled. "I'll stick to the keyboard."

After a few performances, the hostess took the mic. "Come on! Who's next?" she asked.

A family in the back shouted, "Right here! This one!"

The hostess said, "Oh, I think we have someone who's a little shy! Let's give this young lady a little encouragement, huh?" Everyone clapped and hooted. Eventually a small, thin middle-school girl emerged. Her light auburn hair fell partially over the pale hand that shielded her face. She was wearing khaki pants, a buttery-yellow cardigan, and a white T-shirt, as well as a silk scarf with pinks and the yellow of the cardigan. She looked shy and embarrassed.

"That's Claire Roberts from school!" Olivia said.

"She just started at Lakeview at the end of last year. She's from Australia or somewhere. She's so sweet." Olivia waved, but Claire was too busy hiding to see her.

"Claire Roberts doing karaoke?" Robbie said. "I don't think I've ever even heard her voice. She never speaks in class."

"She doesn't have to; she already knows every-thing," Tig said. "She's, like, a genius or something. A real brain."

"She's sweet, though," Olivia repeated. "Don't you think she's sweet?"

"Yeah, she's nice," Tig said. "It's just that nobody really knows her. She's so quiet."

"What's she going to sing?" Robbie asked. "Man, I almost feel bad for her. She looks so embarrassed."

The music started.

It wasn't what they expected.

Heavy guitar and drums. A distinctive riff.

" 'Plush'!" Robbie shouted to Tig. "She's going to sing 'Plush'?"

Claire didn't look at the audience but kept her eyes glued to the screen. She started off quietly, her voice a little shaky. But as the song went on, she got louder.

And gravelly-er.

And rocking-er.

Robbie, Olivia, Kyra, and Tig looked at one another in utter disbelief.

No way! Robbie mouthed to Tig.

Claire Roberts—shy, quiet, little Claire Roberts, who was as delicate as expensive china and seemed like she might break into a million pieces if you looked at her the wrong way—was belting out Stone Temple Pilots as though a rock goddess were trapped inside her tiny body, screaming to escape. Claire seemed to have forgotten that anyone else was in the room and, infected by the music, she belted out the lyrics from a dark, secret place. Never in a million years would Tig or anyone else have guessed that a voice like that—a voice so raw and fierce and commanding— could come out of the cutesy little package all tied up with a yellow-and-pink scarf.

When Claire went back to her seat to the sound of thunderous applause, Robbie stared at Tig. Her eyes were insistent.

"Way ahead of you," Tig said to Robbie.

Chapter Fifteen

"**W**e should've asked her to sit with us," Robbie said as soon as the girls piled into the minivan.

"Not the right moment," Tig said. "Not yet."

"Well, when *is* the right moment?" Robbie asked. "We've *got* to get her. We've just got to. I can already picture the five of us onstage together!"

"First we've got to get rid of Haley," Tig said.

"Who's got Haley's number?" Robbie said. "Kyra, you've probably got it in your phone, right? Gimme."

"Cool your jets, Chan," Tig said. "We can't just call her and blurt out, 'You're out of the band.' "

"Sure we can," Robbie replied. "It's easy. Repeat after me: 'Haley, you're out of the band.' See? Simple." Tig just looked at her. "Well, it's easy for me. Tell you what . . . I'll be glad to do the honors."

"I just bet you would," Tig said with a smile.

Robbie grinned. "Granted, I might be prone to a bit of elaboration. How's this sound? 'Haley, because you're a horrible, spoiled tyrant none of us can stand, we hereby kick you, with great pleasure, out of Pandora's Box. Go forth and stink somewhere else.'"

Even Kyra laughed. But then she added, "If we don't handle this just right, Haley, Regan, and Sofia will go on the warpath."

Robbie scoffed. "They can just bring it, then. I'm not scared of them."

"Oh, I am," Olivia said. "I'm terrified of them!" No one said anything. "What? I'm the only one?"

"Of course not," Tig said. "Robbie, I'd love to be as brave as you are, but the truth is, these girls are vicious, and I'm just not a fighter by nature. I don't like conflict. I'm going to avoid it if I can."

"You're going to let the Bots walk all over you?" Robbie said.

"I didn't say that," Tig said. "Look, I'll break the news to Haley. On Monday. And I'll do it as nicely as I can to try to keep the peace. I don't want it to look like we're dumping Haley for someone else."

"But we are," Olivia said. "We're dumping her for Claire."

"That doesn't mean it has to look like it," Tig replied. "And besides, we were going to dump Haley anyway. It just so happens we found her replacement earlier than we'd anticipated. But if the Bots think we kicked Haley out because of Claire—man, just think what they'd do to poor Claire! And she's so nice. I don't think it would be fair of us to put her in that position."

"It's kind of, like, let's say you were dating this guy who you decide is totally wrong for you," Kyra explained. "And you're planning to break up with him. But before you get a chance, you meet this other great guy who's totally right for you. But you can't go out with Right Guy immediately after you dump Wrong

Guy because then it looks like you dumped Wrong Guy for Right Guy, even though you knew you were going to dump Wrong Guy before you even met Right Guy. Right?"

"Yes," Tig said. "As ridiculously confusing as that was, yes. That's it exactly."

"So we're going to all this trouble to prevent a Botpocalypse from raining down, not only on all of us, but also on Claire?" Robbie asked.

"Yeah," Tig said.

"I guess I can see your point," Robbie replied. "I mean, they can bring it all day long as far as I'm concerned, but Claire does seem fragile. She's so quiet. She might curl up and die if they pick on her. I wouldn't want that. The only part I hate is that we have to be nice about it all to Haley. She certainly doesn't give a rip about being nice to *us*."

"I know," Tig said. "Haley doesn't deserve it. But my mom always says the people who need kindness most are the ones who deserve it least."

"Gag. Did she read that on a poster?" Robbie asked.

"I know," Tig said. "But even so, we've got to be smart about this. Staying out of a war with Haley is a matter of survival. Getting on the wrong side of the Bots would be a *real* Pandora's box that I do *not* want to open if we can avoid it."

"Okay, I can respect that," Robbie said. "It's less fun this way, but I respect it."

"What if Claire says no?" Kyra asked. "I mean, she seemed pretty nervous just getting up for karaoke at Pepe's. What if she doesn't want to be the lead singer for an actual band?"

"It can't hurt to ask," Olivia said. "All she can say is no, and then we're no worse off than we were before."

"Oh, but Claire just has to say yes," Robbie said. "Her voice will haunt my dreams until the day I die!"

"She is amazing," Tig said. "I don't think she realizes how amazing she is. You're right, Robbie. She has to say yes. She just has to."

Chapter Sixteen

Tig had rehearsed her speech to Haley a thousand times over the weekend. She was going to go with the old it's-not-you-it's-me routine: *Your voice is really special, Haley, but we're just not the best band for it. We're more of a rock band, and really, your voice is so much better suited to ballads and pieces where you can really showcase your range.* Sure, it was a snow job, but it was a snow job of kindness and restraint . . . and self-preservation. Tig was sure any reasonable person would appreciate how delicately she handled the situation and would bow out gracefully, self-esteem intact, and not start a war over it.

But, of course, Haley was not known for being a reasonable person.

Tig approached the Bot Spot in the gym Monday morning before school.

In her peripheral vision, she could see Kyra, Olivia, and Robbie sitting together, trying to pretend they weren't watching.

All the Bots in the radius eyed Tig's intrusion into their space with curiosity. No one had to say a word; the knowledge that an outsider had encroached upon their space was instantly telegraphed to them all, and they sat alert, as though awaiting their cue to attack and defend their territory.

"S'up, Haley?" Tig said, trying to sound casual, trying to act as though she didn't feel all those pairs of eyes burning holes through her.

"I suppose you've come to tell me you've gotten rid of that loser who was playing guitar in my band?" Haley said.

Tig felt her face flush. Loser? *Her* band? There

were so many things to be angry about at once, Tig almost couldn't process them. *Keep your head, Tig*, she told herself.

"Actually, I did want to discuss something with you about the band," Tig said. "Could we talk somewhere privately?"

"Anything you have to say to Haley, you can say to our whole crew," Regan said.

Who asked you? Tig wanted to say. "Well, it's kind of a sensitive matter."

"Like Regan said," Haley replied, "whatever you've got to say, spill it."

"Okay, then," Tig said. "About the band. We think your singing is really . . . something. Really something . . . special." Tig wasn't exactly lying. *Special* could mean many things. Like, out of the ordinary. And Haley's singing was definitely out of the ordinary.

Haley beamed and looked at Regan for affirmation.

"So, based on that," Tig continued, "we feel that our band isn't really showcasing your . . . specialness."

"Finally!" Haley said. "It's about time you came to

your senses. So, here's the plan. From now on, I pick the songs, I pick the tempo and the key, and the rest of you basically just do what I tell you. It's going to be a lot better this way."

"That's not exactly what I . . . what we . . . had in mind," Tig said.

Regan bristled. She actually sat up straighter and inclined her face toward Tig. "Then what *did* you have in mind?"

"Well, I . . . we . . . were thinking that maybe Pandora's Box isn't a good fit for Haley's voice. We sort of want to go with more of a rock 'n' roll format, and Haley really needs . . ." Suddenly Tig couldn't remember anything she had rehearsed. She desperately wanted to either erase the entire conversation or end her last sentence with *a lobotomy*, but she knew neither was a viable option.

"Wait," Regan said. "Wait, wait, wait, wait, wait!" She put her hand up and her head down. When she looked back up, she was laughing. But not in a good way. More like an evil villain way. "Are you trying to say

that you . . . that your pathetic little bandmates and
you . . . are kicking Haley out?"

"It's not really like that," Tig said. "'Kicking out'
sounds so harsh. It's more like, I don't know, a
parting of the ways, you might say. We're just going in
different artistic directions." *That sounded pretty good*,
Tig thought. *Not bad*.

But Regan and Haley weren't buying it.

"I cannot *believe* what I'm hearing!" Haley said.
"Who do you think you are? How dare you! How dare
you kick *me* out of your crappy little excuse for a band
when I am the *only* one with any actual talent!"

That was it.

"Look, Haley," Tig said. "I was trying to be nice
about this, but . . ." Tig let out a growl of frustration.
"You just can't let anyone be nice, can you? Okay, then,
fine. Gloves off. The fact is, you can't sing. You can't! I
wish you could, but you can't!" Tig had completely lost
her cool, and people all over the gym were looking at
her. She saw several girls from different cliques whispering to one another. Tig wondered if they thought

she was a psycho or if they admired her for standing up to the Bots.

Haley didn't yell, though. She was quiet. Calm. She said matter-of-factly, "You are an idiot. An ugly, reject, loser idiot. I'm a great singer." She even had a smile on her face when she said it. Anyone watching might have thought Haley had said something nice to Tig. That only made Tig angrier.

"No, you're not!" Tig said. "Maybe these fake friends of yours say you are, maybe your mom and your grandma or whoever says so. But guess what? They're totally lying! You stink! Maybe if you weren't so arrogant, you could learn how to actually sing . . . take some direction from somebody . . . but that's never going to happen! You're condescending and mean and impossible to get along with! So that's it—you're out. Good-bye and good riddance!"

As Tig walked away, adrenaline surging through her body, Regan got up, grabbed Tig's arm, and whispered, "Watch your back!" before returning to her seat.

Olivia, Kyra, and Robbie were staring, open-mouthed, at Tig as she walked up. "I think it's safe to say that didn't go as well as I'd hoped," Tig said.

"We couldn't hear, but it seemed to escalate pretty quickly," Robbie replied.

The four of them looked back at Regan and Haley's stronghold. They were all huddled together in a strategy session.

"This is bad," Kyra said. "What are they going to do to us?"

"I don't know," Tig answered. "But whatever it is, it's not going to be pretty."

Chapter Seventeen

*U*gly.

The word kept rattling around inside Tig's head for the rest of the day and into the evening, taunting her even as she tried to fall asleep that night.

Haley had called her ugly.

Idiot, loser, reject—whatever. She'd expected those. She didn't take them personally. They were just words. Tig knew she wasn't an idiot. She made good grades and was obviously bright. And loser and reject, well, those were just middle-school categories she knew she had it in her to break free from.

But ugly? That stung.

Tig looked in the mirror after supper that night. She examined everything about herself. Her skin was sallow, not radiant. Her nose was kind of a blob. The braces didn't do much for her smile. Her hair was brown and a little on the frizzy side, nothing lush and beautiful about it. She wasn't overweight, but she wasn't skinny. Her legs were thin but not shapely; she disliked her ankles. Her arms were too hairy, her feet too big, her stomach too round.

The only thing she couldn't find fault with were her eyes. They were a greenish-blue, framed by long, dark, thick, curly lashes. They had an interesting shape and setting. They looked sleepy but sparkly at the same time.

At least she had pretty eyes.

As Tig cried herself to sleep that night, she was glad it was her secret. She'd die before she'd ever let Haley Thornton know she'd made her cry.

The band was going to work. She was going to recruit Claire, and then Haley and everyone else would see how awesome an all-girl band could be. Probably they'd become famous one day, and Tig would get her own stylist and makeup artist and all that stuff, and she'd be in magazines that would talk about how pretty she was, how she had such beautiful eyes. They could do all kinds of things with hair and makeup. She'd seen all the before-they-were-famous pics of celebrities; she knew.

And Haley would be standing in the checkout line at the grocery store with her ten screaming kids, and she'd see Tig's beautiful photograph smiling at her from the cover of *Glamour*, and she'd burn with envy. And the story inside the magazine would be all about how Tig hadn't been home to Alabama in years because she was so busy with her tours and recording sessions and her houses in Malibu and New York and Paris. But of course, she would send her private jet occasionally to fly out her family and close friends from school for visits and concerts. And Haley would wish she had been one of those friends from school, but no, she'd blown her chance, and she couldn't get on Tig's jet even if she begged her. She just had to stay in Alabama and live her sad little life as someone completely unfamous and unimportant.

And then they'd just see who was ugly, wouldn't they?

Chapter Eighteen

A full week had passed since Tig had kicked Haley out of the band. Tig kept waiting for the Bots to strike, but the Bots had so far been eerily quiet, showing no signs of an impending attack. That made Tig even more nervous. She was more of a hurry-up-and-rip-off-the-bandage-and-get-it-over-with kind of girl than a drag-out-the-agony type.

Robbie had suggested that the best way for Tig and the other girls to stop worrying about what the Bots might be up to was to learn a new song, and Robbie knew just the one: "Plush," of course.

The basic beat of "Plush" was so different from "Sweet Home Alabama," it took Tig a full hour just to get the coordination down. She could practically do the *one and, three and* bass kick for "SHA" in her sleep, but this song required the kick on *one and*, the *and* of two, and the *and* of three. And that was just the basic beat; the orchestral ruff before the lyrics started was basically a sophisticated flam that required her to hold the sticks differently than she was used to in order to bounce the left stick so that it hit the snare three times in one beat.

But Robbie was so enamored of the song, and Claire's voice singing it, Tig had vowed to try. Robbie wanted them to be able to play the song by the time Claire joined the band, which, as far as Robbie was concerned, couldn't come soon enough.

Tig was so focused on the ruff, she didn't hear Mrs. Freeman call her name three times before she snatched the pencils out of Tig's hands.

"Antigone, for the purposes of this class, pencils are for writing," Mrs. Freeman said.

"Yes, ma'am," Tig replied. The class giggled.

Sofia was in the class with her and rolled her eyes but made no comment. Kyra and Tig looked at each other. They'd both been on edge, waiting for Haley, Regan, and Sofia to strike.

When class was over, Claire was still zipping up her binder while the other students were filing out the door.

Tig elbowed Kyra. "Hey, Claire," Tig said. "How's it going?"

Claire smiled demurely. "Good."

"So, we caught your act at Pepe's a couple of weekends ago," Tig said.

"Yeah, you were really good!" Kyra added. "We were wondering . . ."

Tig cleared her throat and gave Kyra a stern look. She'd already discussed with Kyra how this would work. First they'd make friends with Claire. Then Tig would ask her to join the band.

"We were wondering if you enjoyed yourself," Tig said.

Claire blushed. "Oh, my brother made me do it,"

she said. "I was so embarrassed!" She definitely had an accent, but whether it was Australian or English, Tig couldn't quite tell.

"Well, you shouldn't be," Tig said. "You were great."

"Thanks," Claire said. "I just get nervous having all those people look at me."

"Say, where do you sit in the lunch room?" Tig asked.

"Usually over by the outside doors," Claire said.

"Well, if you ever want to sit with us, we have room," Tig said.

"Really? Okay, thanks."

As the three girls walked out of English class together, Tig saw Haley, Regan, and Sofia eyeing them from down the corridor.

"See you at lunch," Tig said as she and Kyra turned to go opposite from Claire and away from the staring Bots.

"I still don't see why we're going to all this trouble," Kyra said. "Why can't we just go ahead and ask Claire to be in the band?"

"Because we don't want to spook her," Tig said. "It would be like some guy you just met asking you out."

"You say that like it would be a bad thing."

"Besides, Claire said she was embarrassed about being onstage. If we ask her now, she'll say no. But once we're all friends, it won't be this big, scary proposition—it'll be this cool activity good friends do together as a sort of project."

"So we're going to manipulate her?"

"It's not manipulation," Tig said. "Not if our motives are pure. Claire seems really nice. But she's shy. Let's get to know her, see if we all click. We know she's got the pipes, but as we've recently learned, bands need to work well as a team. Let's see if we all mesh together. We can't risk getting another uncooperative diva out front. We need someone we all actually like. Someone who's a team player."

"With her voice, she could spit in Robbie's face and Robbie would still want her singing lead," Kyra said.

"Claire doesn't strike me as the face-spitting type," Tig replied.

"Me neither. She really does seem sweet."

"Kyra, do me a favor. Keep this under your hat."

"I won't say a word!"

"I mean it this time," Tig said. "Just because we haven't heard from Regan's crew yet about the incident with Haley doesn't mean we won't. In fact, it worries me more that it's taking them so long to strike. Like they're cooking up something really big."

"Maybe they're not going to do anything at all," said Kyra. When Tig rolled her eyes, Kyra said, "I know. Wishful thinking."

"Regan won't let a challenge to the order go unpunished," Tig said. "Girls like her don't get to the top and stay there by letting girls like us defy them. No, something's coming. The best thing we can do right now is to be ready and make sure they don't have any new information to use against us. Got it?"

Kyra promised to be discreet.

Tig would work on wooing Claire. And on getting "Plush" figured out.

And in the meantime, she'd watch her back.

Chapter Nineteen

Claire joined Tig and the other girls at the lunch table the next day.

Tig had already instructed the other members of the band not to pounce. "Get to know her," Tig had told them. "Just be cool."

"So tell us about yourself," Tig said to Claire. "Where'd you come from?"

"Yeah, Mars or Jupiter?" Robbie said. Claire laughed quietly.

"That did sound weird," Tig said. "What I meant was, where did you live before you moved here?"

"England," Claire said.

"That's so cool!" Olivia said.

"We were kinda wondering about the accent," Tig said. "It's awesome."

"That's one nice benefit of living in the States," Claire said. "Americans are easily charmed by any rubbish that comes out of my mouth, it seems." She smiled.

"Have you ever been to Wimbledon?" Olivia asked.

"I'm afraid not."

"I plan on playing there one day!" Olivia said.

"Oh, wouldn't that be lovely?" Claire replied.

"Lovely!" Olivia said with a big smile. "That sounds so . . . British! You have such a cool accent! I bet you could talk your way out of anything around here!"

"How'd you end up in Alabama, of all places, from England?" Will asked.

"My dad accepted a position at the university. He's heading up one of the English department's programs on Shakespeare."

Kyra asked, "Do you miss England? Do you ever

get to go back to visit?"

"Our plan is to go home about once a year," Claire replied. "Over the holidays to visit family."

"England and Alabama," Tig said. "That's an interesting combination."

"Yeah," Claire said. "Should make for an odd blending of accents. Dad's already teasing me about picking up a Southern drawl. I'm probably the only person in town who says *mum* in one breath and *y'all* in the next!"

Tig loved the idea of having a new friend who was British. It seemed so exotic.

"What's your favorite part about England?" Kyra asked.

"Definitely the shopping," Claire said. "Not to say that the old beautiful castles and such aren't wonderful to visit, but really, some of the shops back home are to die for!"

As Claire and the other girls chatted about shopping in England, Tig felt someone staring at her. She looked up to see Haley, Regan, and Sofia watching from their table. When they saw Tig look at them, they looked away and began what looked to Tig like plotting. Tig told herself to ignore them . . . at least for now.

"So what kind of music do you like?" Tig asked Claire.

"Oh, really anything," Claire said. "I love all sorts of music."

"Yeah, us too," Tig said. "All of us do, in fact. You should come over sometime. The girls and I have this, well, you might call it a musical community. We get together at my house—my family has this little building on our property, and my folks let me use it as kind of a hangout, so sometimes we jam a little bit."

"You all have a band?" Claire asked.

"Well, you could call it a band," Tig said. "It's no big, really. Very casual. We just kind of mess around."

"Tig's the drummer," Will said.

"You've heard her play?" said Claire.

"Not yet," Will replied. "But I'd like to."

"Will just wants to make fun of how pathetic I

am," Tig said, smiling. "But he's not going to get the chance."

"I might not make fun," Will said. "Depends on how badly you play."

The moment had come. Tig was just about to invite Claire over to her house Friday night when a shadow fell over the table.

"I absolutely *love* that scarf!" It was Haley. She was looking right at Claire.

"Oh, thank you," Claire replied.

"You're in my study hall, aren't you?" Haley asked.

"Yes, I think so."

"I'm Haley."

"I know," Claire said. "I'm Claire."

"You're new, right?"

"Kind of."

"Well, it's great to meet you. Come sit with me in study hall, okay?"

"Sure," Claire said. "I'd like that."

As Haley walked away, Robbie, Tig, Olivia, and Kyra exchanged a look.

Tig rolled her eyes and turned her attention back to Claire. "So, as I was saying, we're getting together Friday night if you want to come."

"Wasn't that nice of Haley to come over and introduce herself?" Claire replied.

"Sure," Tig said.

"I wonder what she's like," Claire said.

"I'd be happy to answer that question for you," Robbie said.

Tig shot her a look. "We don't really know her all that well," Tig said. "So, what about Friday night? Want to join us?"

"I'd like that," Claire said. "I don't play an instrument, so I'd love to see you all play."

"Great," Tig said. "Let's make it a slumber party! We have those all the time at my house. It's tons of fun."

"What time should I be there?" Will asked.

Robbie gave Will a playful smack on the head. "You wish!"

Will laughed. "Can't blame a guy for trying."

"Sounds good," Claire said. "I'll ask my mum and let you know tomorrow."

Tig tried not to scream *Yes!* and high-five Robbie. She could hardly wait to get home and work some more on "Plush." Claire was going to be their lead singer. Claire didn't know it yet, of course, but Tig could just feel it.

Chapter Twenty

It came as no surprise that even Claire's pajamas were classic: pale pink cotton with the traditional collar and four buttons on top, and white piping along the collar, pants, and sleeves. She accessorized with small pearl stud earrings and the same baby-pink color of polish on her toes.

In contrast, Robbie wore a gray-and-white tie-dyed Pink Floyd T-shirt and boxer shorts; Olivia, Hello Kitty pj pants and a tee from a tennis tournament; and Tig and Kyra, supersoft yoga pants and tees from last year's fall festival at school.

Tig half expected Claire to pull out a satin sleep mask to complete her look—but if she had, Tig wouldn't have minded. It would have suited Claire. There was something about her Tig admired. The way she carried herself with natural elegance. Tig wondered how she learned it, or if it wasn't something that could be learned but was instead a gift from birth. Or if it was just a product of being British.

They'd had a good evening so far. They'd ordered pizza, watched a few reruns of *I Love Lucy*, and even done a few hilarious impressions of teachers and the principal (he was easy—all Tig had to do was nonchalantly throw around gigantic vocabulary words). They'd hung out for a while in the studio, showing Claire their instruments and playing "Sweet Home Alabama" for her . . . but not "Plush." It wasn't time. Tig had warned the other girls not to "scare the fish"; and besides, Kyra and Tig still didn't have the whole thing down yet.

"So what do you think of Lakeview Heights so far, Claire?" Olivia asked.

"I like it," Claire said. "For a while I wasn't so sure. I'm not the best at making friends, and at first no one really talked to me. But now I'm friends with you all, and I'm getting on well with Haley in my study hall, too. She's been really nice."

Tig felt ice water speed through her veins. "Haley?"

"Yes," Claire said. "In fact, she invited me to the movies with her group tonight, but of course, I'd already made plans with you. It was rather nice to feel socially desirable, though. Imagine . . . here I am choosing between two lovely sets of friends!"

"Isn't it funny how Haley took an interest in you just about the time you started sitting with us at lunch?" Robbie asked.

The suggestion of sarcasm was lost on Claire. "Quite," she said. "I suppose you all are good luck!"

"Robbie, can you give me a hand with the popcorn?" Tig asked.

Once the two of them were in the kitchen, Tig said to Robbie, "Don't go there about Haley."

"Why not?" Robbie said. "Somebody should warn

Claire."

"If we trash Haley, we'll just look petty and mean, and Claire won't want to be friends with us. Let's take the high road."

"You and your high road. Fine, whatever you say."

When Robbie and Tig returned with popcorn, the only lights were from the humming television and the streetlight outside the living room window. "What do y'all want to do now?" Tig asked as she picked up a skinny slice of cold pizza from the box and nibbled the crust.

"We could look at funny YouTube videos," Kyra offered halfheartedly. No one bit.

"We could play a game," Olivia suggested.

"Not video tennis," Kyra said. "You'd have an unfair advantage."

Olivia grinned. "How about a dance-off? I brought that new dance challenge game."

"Count me out," Robbie said.

"Yeah, me too," said Tig.

"Got any other games?" Olivia asked.

It was quiet for a moment before Robbie said, "I know a game!" Her smile said it was going to be either really bad or really fun . . . or maybe both.

"If this involves sneaking out to TP Mrs. Freeman's yard, the answer is still no," Tig said. "I already told you: it's too obvious, and we'd get busted in a heartbeat."

"Besides, I like Mrs. Freeman," Olivia said.

"I like her, too," Robbie said. "But what's that got to do with it? She's a teacher. It's almost our sacred duty to mess with her. But Tig's right. We'd get busted. Besides, it's almost too . . ."

"Pedestrian?" Claire said.

"Yeah," Robbie said.

Kyra said, "Whatever that means."

Claire blushed. "You know, like banal."

Kyra laughed. "Thanks for clearing that up."

Now Claire really blushed and put her hand over her eyes and laughed at herself. "Sorry! I actually like vocabulary. Over the summer I look up a new word every day. I know—I'm a total nerd."

"I don't think that's nerdy," said Tig. "I think that's really cool. And even cooler that you told us."

Claire smiled. "So, what do you have in mind for us, Robbie?"

"Like I always say, if it ain't broke, don't fix it," Robbie replied.

"Fix what? And since when do you always say that?" Tig said.

"Since now," Robbie said. "Slumber party games, I mean. Don't reinvent the wheel; go with a classic. An oldie but a goodie. How about Truth or Dare?"

Kyra clapped her hands. "Ooh! I haven't played that in years!"

Olivia said, "Sounds fun."

"Okay by me," said Tig. "What do you think, Claire?"

"Sure. Whatever you all want to do."

"Let's go up to my room. The walls have ears." Tig gestured toward the kitchen, where her mom and dad were cleaning up paper plates and gathering the garbage.

Tig's room was painted a silvery blue, which made her white wooden furniture and zebra-print bedding pop. Tig shut and locked the door, and the five girls piled onto her bed. "Who's first?" Tig asked, grabbing a pillow to hug.

"Since it was Robbie's idea, she gets to decide," Kyra suggested.

"Okay, then," Robbie said. "Claire, truth or dare?"

"No, don't make Claire go first," Tig said. "She barely knows us. We can't expect her to spill her secrets."

"Right," Kyra said. "At least not until she has enough dirt on us to ensure our secrecy!"

"All right, all right," Robbie said. "Olivia. Truth or dare?"

Olivia pursed her lips and looked up at the ceiling. "Truth!"

"Chicken!" Kyra teased.

"If you could date any guy at school," Robbie said, "who would it be?"

Olivia grinned. "Promise you won't tell a soul?"

"And break the sanctity of the sleepover?" Tig said. "Perish the thought!"

"Then I'll tell you," Olivia said. "You promise, right?"

"Just spit it out!" Kyra said, elbowing Olivia.

"Okay, okay, okay," Olivia said. "Will."

"No way!" Robbie said. Kyra squealed in delight.

"Will Mason?" Tig asked.

"You promised you wouldn't tell!" Olivia said. "A promise is a promise!"

Tig furrowed her brow. "Of course I won't tell," she said. "But just . . . Will? Really?"

"He's adorable!" Olivia said. "Don't you think so, Kyra?"

"Sure," Kyra said. "Adorable. Right, Tig?"

"I guess I've just never thought of Will as, you know, adorable or whatever," Tig replied. "Don't you think he's kind of annoying?"

"Not at all!" Olivia said. "Have you ever looked at those eyes?" She threw herself dramatically back onto the bed. "I could get lost in those eyes!"

"Will does have nice eyes," Claire said. "He seems like a nice fellow." She looked at Tig. "Isn't he?"

"Well, yeah," Tig said. "I mean, I guess so. It's just . . . Will? Really? Will Mason?"

Olivia hit Tig's arm playfully. "Yes, Will Mason!"

Tig looked at Robbie. "Will Mason is adorable?"

"I don't do adorable," said Robbie. "Not my thing. But whatever works for you, Olivia. Okay, you're next."

"Tig," Olivia said. "Truth or dare?"

Tig's mind was reeling from Olivia's revelation. She could barely think straight. Olivia liked Will? Why? And how long had she been crushing on him? And why did Tig care? She didn't care. She totally didn't care. "Dare," she said.

Olivia smiled. "I dare you to call Will," she said, "on speakerphone! And find out what he thinks of me!"

Robbie high-fived Olivia. "Way to take the bull by the horns!" she said. "I mean, the more direct bull-and-horns method would be to just woman up and ask him yourself and then tell him to get lost if you don't like his answer, but you know, this could work, too."

"I don't know about this, y'all," Tig said.

"You have to do it! It's a dare!" Olivia said.

"Yeah, but what if you don't like what he says?"

"You think Will doesn't like me?"

"I don't know. I'm not saying that. Look, I'll take the dare if it's something I have to do, but it's not really fair to Will to put him on speakerphone without telling him."

Claire said, "That's true. It would be bad form."

"But I'm *dying* to know!" Olivia said.

"How long have you liked Will, anyway?" Kyra asked.

"Since the beginning of the year," Olivia replied. "Did you see him when he got back from the beach this summer? His hair was so shiny, with the highlights from the sun, and his cute little legs were all brown."

Tig hadn't noticed.

"How about a compromise?" Robbie suggested. "How about if Tig calls him but doesn't put him on speakerphone? She can make inquiries for you, get you the info you want, but not put Will in a bad position.

That's fair, don't you think, Tig?"

Tig took a deep breath. "I guess so."

"Yay!" Olivia said. "Call him right now!"

"I don't even know his number."

"It's on his profile page," Olivia said. "Not that I've cyberstalked him. Much."

Once they had the number, Olivia, Robbie, Claire, and Kyra positioned themselves on the bed around Tig and stared as she started dialing. Tig stopped. "You're all creeping me out."

"It's just so exciting!" Olivia said. "I want to know what he says."

"Well, I can't work under this kind of pressure," Tig said. "I'm taking the phone into the bathroom." The girls whined. "Don't worry; I'll give you a full report."

Tig barricaded herself in the bathroom, sitting on a fuzzy bath mat. She took another deep breath as the number she called started ringing.

"Hello?"

"Will?"

"Yes. Who's this?"

"Tig. Tig Ripley."

"Oh. For a second there I thought maybe it was Tig Smith or Tig Finkleheimer."

Tig laughed. "I guess that was a bit redundant."

"Well, Tig Ripley, what's up?"

"Yes," Tig said. "What is up, indeed." What? What did she just say? What in the heck did that even mean?

Will laughed. "I don't know. You tell me."

"I just, you know, wanted to see what you were up to."

"Just watching TV. How about you?"

"Nothing much. Just sitting here in my bathroom."

"You don't say?" replied Will.

Tig realized how weird that sounded. "I mean, I'm not sitting in the bathroom, like, you know, using it or anything. I'm just in here because . . . my phone gets better reception in here."

"Okay," Will said.

"So, I just thought we could, you know, chat."

"Sounds good. What do you want to chat about?"

Tig made small talk about the drums for a few minutes. Will seemed to enjoy the conversation.

He told her about a song he was learning and asked how her lessons were going. It was nice, and Tig kind of forgot why she'd called him in the first place . . . until Olivia opened the door and mouthed, *What?* and waved her hands around.

Tig shooed her out and this time locked the door behind her.

"Will," Tig said. "I have a question for you."

"Shoot."

"Do you like anyone at school?"

"I might," Will replied. "I might even like someone at our lunch table."

"Who?"

"That's for me to know and you to find out."

"Seriously?" Tig said. "That's the best you could come up with?"

Will laughed. "That was pretty bad."

Maybe she should take a different approach. "What do you think of Olivia?"

"Olivia?" Will asked. "Great tennis player, and I think she's a nice girl. Everybody thinks so."

"You think she's nice?"

"Yeah. Sweet girl."

Someone knocked at the bathroom door. "Cool," Tig said. "I gotta go." She hung up before Will could even say good-bye.

Tig threw open the door. *"What?"*

"I'm sorry!" Olivia said. "We couldn't stand it any longer! What took you so long?"

"I didn't want to seem obvious!"

"What did he say? Does he like me?"

Tig went back to the bed. Olivia followed. "He said you're sweet."

Olivia's face lit up. "Sweet? He used the exact word *sweet?*" Tig nodded. "Oh, my gosh, y'all! Will Mason thinks I'm sweet!" Olivia squealed and hugged Kyra.

"What else did he say?" Kyra asked.

"That was pretty much it."

"All that time on the phone and that's what you got?" Robbie asked.

"Did you ask him if he likes her?" Claire said. "You know—*likes* her, likes her?"

"Not exactly," Tig said.

"What does 'not exactly' mean?" said Olivia. "Did you ask him or not?"

"I was trying, but I didn't get that far before you banged on the door!"

"Right," Olivia said. "Shoot. I should've been more patient." She pondered the news a moment. "Sweet is good, isn't it?"

"Of course sweet is good," Robbie said. "I mean, for you. Not for me, of course. I don't do sweet."

"Or adorable," Claire reminded her.

"Precisely."

Olivia's demeanor suddenly changed. "No, no, no, no, no," she said. "This isn't good. Sweet isn't good."

"How can sweet not be good?" asked Kyra.

"Sweet is bland. Sweet is baby kittens or your grandmother. Sweet is not pretty. Oh, this is awful. It's just like last year when all the guys signed my yearbook the same way."

"What way?" asked Claire.

"Every guy in the sixth grade wrote the same thing

in my yearbook: *Olivia, you are the nicest girl in school. Good luck with tennis!*"

"That's so sweet!" Kyra said.

"Kyra," Olivia said. "Don't you realize that's guy code for 'You will die alone'? No one wants to date sweet. Guys want to date hot. Like Regan."

"But Regan's . . ." Tig was going to say something mean but stopped herself because of Claire. "Self-assured. Most guys we know wouldn't even approach her."

"They still all want to date her," said Olivia.

That was true. What was it about guys that drew them to mean, stuck-up girls like Regan?

"Let's face it," said Olivia. "I'm doomed."

"Don't be ridiculous," Claire said. "You're quite fetching, Olivia. You have beautiful hair and cute freckles. And there's nothing wrong with being sweet. Nothing at all."

"I guess so," Olivia said.

"Hey, if Will doesn't like you, someone else with better taste will," Robbie said.

"I don't want anyone else to like me," Olivia said. "I just want Will."

"Enough about Will," Tig said. And really, she'd had enough. Since when was Will so important? He sat with them every single day at lunch, and she'd never thought a thing about him. She'd certainly never thought any of the other girls had. She'd have to process this information later, when she could be alone with her thoughts. "I believe it's my turn! Kyra! Truth or dare?"

"You already know all my secrets," Kyra said. "So how about a dare?"

After much deliberation—and suggestions from the other girls—Tig dared Kyra to eat a tablespoon of mayonnaise. Kyra absolutely *hated* mayo, so this was a big dare. It took about fifteen minutes for her to choke down only about a teaspoon, and the girls finally just called it even, not wanting Kyra to barf all over them.

After she rinsed the mayo taste out with a glass of sweet tea, it was Kyra's turn. "If Claire's going last, then I guess I'll pick Robbie. Truth or dare?"

"Have we met?"

"What do you mean?" Kyra asked.

"It means," Tig explained, "that Robbie always tells the truth about what she thinks—even when she maybe shouldn't—so there's no reason to ask for truth, and she's fearless enough to do anything, so you might as well give her a dare."

"You complete me, Ripley," Robbie said. "Have I ever told you that?"

"All right, then," Kyra said. "I dare you to . . . I don't know. I can't think of anything."

"I can," Tig said.

"What? What?" asked Kyra.

"She'll kill me if I tell you."

"What is it?" Olivia asked. "Is it a good one?"

"Oh, it's a good one, all right."

"What is it, Ripley?" Robbie said. "Come on. I can take it."

Tig went to her closet and pulled out a printed dress with a lace collar.

"That's the dress your mom bought you for that

wedding last year," Kyra said.

"What do you think of it, Claire?" Tig asked.

"It's very, um . . ."

"Go ahead. You can say it," said Tig.

"It's horrible," Claire said.

Tig replied, "Exactly."

Kyra broke into a huge grin. "Oh, that *is* good!"

"What?" said Robbie. "What's good? You're not suggesting I wear that, are you?"

"Tig did say you were fearless," said Olivia. "Are you *that* fearless?"

"Of course I am. Here, give it to me. I'll put it on."

"Not now," Kyra said. "I dare you to wear it to school on Monday."

Tig started laughing. "Kyra! You are evil! I was just going to say for right now!"

"Where's the fun in that?" Kyra replied. "How about it, Chan? Are you really fearless?"

Robbie walked tentatively to the dress Tig held up. She stroked the brushed cotton and the lace collar, then looked defiantly at the girls. "I'd say this really brings out my purple streak."

Robbie put the dress on top of her overnight bag so she wouldn't forget to take it home with her the next day. "As if I could forget something that ugly," she said. "Good thing I have no reputation to destroy. And good thing for Kyra and Tig that I have a remarkable sense of humor."

"We've got one person left," said Kyra. "But who gets to ask Claire? Robbie's already done one—she did Olivia's truth."

"May I do the honors?" Tig asked.

"Sure," said Claire. "Fire away."

"Truth or dare?"

"Hmmm . . . dare I say dare?" Claire asked. "How many more hideous dresses do you have in that closet of yours?"

Tig smiled. "Robbie took the last one."

"Lucky me," Robbie said.

"Then dare," Claire replied.

"This wasn't how I'd planned to do this," Tig said. "But since we're in the mode, I'm going to go for it."

Robbie, Kyra, and Olivia nodded.

"What are you up to?" Claire asked.

"Claire, that night at Pepe's, we were totally blown away. You're amazing. We invited you to sit with us at lunch and to hang with us tonight because we wanted to know if you were as amazing as your voice. We think you are. You're smart and talented and nice and just all-around supercool."

"Wow," said Claire. "Thanks. What's this all about?"

"I dare you," Tig said, "to join our band as the lead singer."

Claire let out a tiny gasp. "Really? But I don't really have a pretty voice."

"That's right," Robbie said. "Your voice isn't pretty. It's primal. Gritty. It's rock 'n' roll, baby!"

"We love your voice," Tig said.

"And we love you!" Olivia added. "Don't we, girls?" Everyone nodded.

"Please say yes," said Kyra. "It will be so much fun! And Robbie will cry if you say no."

"She's right," Robbie said. "I will totally boohoo.

Right here, right now. You don't want that, do you?"

Claire smiled, and her fair skin blushed pink again. "I really don't think I'm much of a singer. Getting up in front of people, having them look at me, listen to me . . . I don't know what to say."

"Say yes!" Tig said. "It will be *killer* fun! All of us together, rocking out! It will kick so much butt, it's not even funny! And we'll help you with the stage fright. We'll work on it with you. Claire, once you got going that night at Pepe's, you owned that stage. You just have to practice. And believe in yourself. And we believe in you so much, you won't be able *not* to believe in yourself."

"Well, it might be fun," Claire said. "How about we give it a try and just see how it goes?"

"Fair enough," Tig said. "If you don't like it, you can quit. No hard feelings. We'll still be your friends."

"Then I say yes," Claire said.

Robbie put her arm around Claire's shoulders and said, "Welcome to Pandora's Box!"

Chapter Twenty-One

First practice was, of necessity, the following morning. It just made sense given that everyone was already there. And besides, Olivia had to leave for tennis before noon.

"Do you know the lyrics to 'Sweet Home Alabama'?" Tig asked Claire once everyone was settled in the studio that morning.

Claire smiled. "How could I live in Alabama for nearly a full year and not know those lyrics?"

"Good point."

Robbie strapped on her guitar, Tig climbed behind

the drum set, Olivia adjusted all of her buttons, Kyra fixed her amp settings, and Claire positioned herself behind the mic. "Here goes nothing," Claire said.

From the moment Robbie began the first riff, Tig could feel the magic in the air. Oh, not to say there weren't a few slipups here and there; there were. But Claire growled out the lyrics from the first note to the last with ferocity. And without a touch of a British accent.

After the first run-through, the five girls stood staring at one another for a minute before anyone said anything.

"Wow," Tig said.

"Was I okay?" Claire asked.

"Were you okay?" Tig repeated. "Were you okay? Um, yeah! If everything were as okay as you, we'd be on the cover of *Rolling Stone* next month!"

"You nailed it," Robbie said.

"So did you, Chan," Tig said.

"Thanks," Robbie replied. "It's just—I don't know. It's tough for one person to match Lynyrd

Skynyrd's three-guitar force."

"True," Tig said. "But where are we going to find two other girls who can play guitar like you?"

"I don't even want to try," Robbie said. "We had enough trouble just getting a lead singer."

"You got that right," Olivia remarked.

"We'll make it work," Robbie said. "Olivia, you tore up that keyboard. Great job."

"Claire's got the lead vocals," Tig said. "But we need somebody besides Olivia to back her up. Olivia can hit those high notes on the chorus, but we need more volume, more depth. We need two voices at least."

The girls looked at one another. Nobody volunteered. "Listen, I'm not much of a singer, especially with high parts," Tig said. "But I can probably do a little bit if Robbie and Kyra do it with me. That way we don't have to have a lot of power behind the backup vocals; we can make up for it with layering the voices."

They agreed to give it a try, even though Kyra, Robbie, and Tig weren't the best singers. They played the song on Tig's iPhone and sang the backup part together a few times before playing the entire song again from the top with the new vocals.

"That wasn't bad," Tig said. "But you can hardly hear our voices. We're going to have to get more microphones and stands. I've got some money saved up. I could get one of those boom mics and hang it over the drums on a stand with a scissor arm."

"I'll spring for one," said Robbie. "Kyra and I can share it."

"Sounds good," Tig said. They agreed to purchase the mics before the next practice. "Let's run through it once more. We'll just have to sing as loud as we can."

They played the song through again. When they finished, they heard someone clapping from outside the studio. They'd left the door open, and Tig's uncle Paul, her dad's brother, peeked through. "Bravo!" he said, still clapping.

"Uncle Paul," Tig said. "What're you doing here?"

"Just stopped in to borrow some pool toys."

Pool toys? "It's too cold for swimming," Tig said. "You're going to make the kids sick."

"It's for a campaign one of my students is doing," Uncle Paul explained. "He needs props for the shoot." Uncle Paul was an advertising professor at the university and often had odd requests for items his students needed in their ads. "Anyway, I heard there was a rock band in concert out here, so I had to check it out. Y'all sound great!"

"Thanks," said Tig. "We've been working on this song for a while."

"Play it again," said Uncle Paul.

The next time through was better still. Kyra dropped the bass line only once and Tig messed up a couple of times on the drums, but they recovered quickly. When it was over, Claire's smile was so big, her eyes nearly disappeared.

"You guys!" she said. "That was so much fun!"

The five of them hugged and high-fived.

"Hey, how'd you like to play your first gig?" Uncle Paul asked.

"Gig?" Tig asked. "This is the only song we know."

"Yeah, but your aunt Kate would love it if you

played her surprise party."

"But Aunt Kate's surprise party is tonight!" Tig said. "And you've already hired a band."

"I'm sure they'd stand aside long enough for you girls to perform this one song. What do you say?"

"Claire?" Tig asked.

"This is all happening so fast," Claire replied. "How many people will be there?"

"It's nobody you'd know," Tig said. "Just a bunch of old people."

"Thanks," said Uncle Paul.

"What's the pay?" Robbie asked.

Uncle Paul grinned. "I like your style," he replied. "How about ten bucks apiece?"

Tig looked at the other girls. Their wide smiles told her they were in.

"I guess I could try," Claire said.

"You've got yourself a deal," Robbie said, shaking Uncle Paul's hand. "Joke's on you, though. We would've done it for free."

"Joke's on you. I would've paid you twenty apiece."

Chapter Twenty-Two

"I'm so excited!" Tig's mom said. "Your first performance! Oh, I hope I don't mess up the timing. Everything has to go perfectly. Kate is going to *flip*! She's going to love your band playing for her." Mom was in charge of getting Kate to the surprise party on time. She was supposed to lure her shopping and make her stay away from her house until five p.m. Tig thought that shouldn't be too hard. Tig's mom and Aunt Kate went shopping together all the time.

The Pandora's Box girls met at Tig's aunt and uncle's house to practice after Olivia's tennis game.

They ran through "Sweet Home" a few times, making sure the mic levels and amps were set up correctly. Pandora's Box was to be the opening act, the first song that began playing when Kate came home to find her surprise party.

Tig's aunt and uncle's house had a big backyard, and her uncle had set it up with tiki torches and strings of clear lights on the gazebo. There was plenty of pulled-pork barbeque, coleslaw, chips, and banana pudding, and canned drinks in galvanized tubs full of ice. A banner said, HAPPY TWENTY-NINTH, KATE!

"I thought you said she was forty?" Tig asked.

"You're too young to understand," Uncle Paul replied.

As people began arriving, Tig stared to feel a little nervous. What if this had been a terrible idea? What if they choked? But one look at Robbie made her fears dissipate. Robbie didn't know what the word *nervous* even meant. She had kicked back in the oversize chair in the den, reading Uncle Paul's copy of some advertising journal. Her right leg was over one armrest, her back against the other. She didn't even sit in chairs like other people. With Robbie on guitar, what could possibly go wrong?

Uncle Paul made an announcement. "They'll be here in five minutes! Everybody, get ready!"

The fifty or so partygoers filed into the backyard and got quiet. Tig sat down behind the drums and gripped the sticks. Olivia perched herself behind the keyboard, Kyra and Robbie strapped on their bass and guitar. Claire, a death grip on the microphone, turned and looked worriedly at Tig. Tig gave her a thumbs-up. They heard a car door slam.

"Can't we do that in a minute?" Kate's voice said.

"No, come around here and show me that new climbing rose bush," Tig's mom said. "I'm dying to see how it looks."

When Aunt Kate and Tig's mom got to the backyard, Kate's mouth dropped open.

"Surprise!" everyone yelled.

"Happy birthday, baby!" Uncle Paul said, hugging his wife.

Then Robbie began that familiar riff, and soon Tig joined in. Claire's voice didn't shake a bit. It all felt so natural. Before Tig knew it, the song was over, and the crowd was cheering.

Uncle Paul took the mic from Claire. "For the first time ever, ladies and gentlemen, Pandora's Box!" More cheers. The girls took bows, then moved out of the way so the real band could take over.

"Sweet pea!" Aunt Kate said, hugging Tig. "I didn't know you had a band! I'm so proud of you! That was just precious!"

When Kate let Tig out of the hug and went back to her friends, Robbie said, "Precious? Did she really just call us precious? Gag."

"Oh, come on," Tig said. "She's an aunt. They have to say stuff like that. Besides, you're just as cute as a button! Yes, you are!" Tig said it in an old lady voice and pinched Robbie's cheek.

Robbie swatted Tig's hand away, but she couldn't help laughing. "Okay, okay. I guess we are pretty precious, aren't we?"

"The preciousest!" Tig said.

Claire, Kyra, and Olivia came over to Tig and Robbie, and they all hugged. "That was so fun!" Claire said. "I wasn't even nervous! Well, after we got started."

"We rocked!" Olivia said.

"Who's the coolest all-girl band in town? We are!" Kyra said. The girls exchanged high fives.

The rest of the night was a blur of congratulations from the adults at the party. Even though it was just a bunch of her aunt and uncle's middle-aged friends, the praise felt good.

I could get used to this, Tig thought.

Chapter Twenty-Three

The glow of Aunt Kate's party had faded by Monday, when Tig had to return to the cold realities of middle school.

Haley's counterattack—if you could consider Tig's kicking her out of the band an attack—was quite brilliant. Even Tig had to admit it.

Mrs. Baker had gotten some sort of a grant to do an anti-bullying campaign in social studies, and they'd been doing worksheets and skits for two weeks about how to stand up to bullies. Now it was time for the culmination of the unit: student essays and presentations about how bullying had personally affected their lives.

Tig did hers on how she'd once witnessed a fight at school and how it was never okay to hit anyone. Kyra's was about a rumor from last year about how she'd had a crush on a guy in their class. She left out the part about how she'd been the one who started the rumor because she had thought it would make him ask her out. It didn't. Robbie's was more of a persuasive essay about how nobody is important enough to make you feel bad about yourself. Mrs. Baker gave her kudos for dressing outrageously to prove her point—even though no one else had dared say a word about the hideous dress Robbie had worn with combat boots to fulfill the dare.

When Haley got up to present her paper, Tig expected a generic, phoned-in essay.

But what she got was a total oh-no-she-didn't moment.

"The Psychology of Bullies," Haley read, "by Haley Thornton." She cleared her throat and continued.

"Bullies pick on people because they feel bad about themselves. They know they are nothing special, so they find people who are special and try to bring them down to their pathetic level.

"Sadly, I became the victim of a vicious bully this year, so I know firsthand how it feels to be treated like dirt by a peer. I won't say her name because I've decided to be the bigger person, but this girl did everything she could to make me feel terrible about myself. She is jealous of me because I'm much prettier than she is and I have lots of friends, while she is ugly and a loser. Yet because I felt sorry for her since no one likes her, I did her a favor and tried to help her with an extracurricular project. I thought maybe I could try to be her friend. But I soon found out there was a reason no one likes her. She rejected my help and yelled a lot of mean things to me in the gym one morning, in front of everyone, just to hurt my feelings. I was so upset to think that anyone could be so horrible, especially after I'd been nothing but nice to her.

"However, I've learned that this unnamed person's issues are her problem, not mine. I refuse to be dragged down to her level by participating in her pettiness. I realize I am special, and no one has the right to make me feel otherwise!"

Haley capped off her speech with a giant smile and a bow.

The class clapped and cheered.

Except, of course, for Tig, Kyra, Robbie, and Will, who sat there stunned.

Mrs. Baker seemed skeptical. "Okay, Haley," she said. "That was interesting. Thank you."

While Mrs. Baker was making a note in her grade book, Haley looked directly at Tig, leaving no doubt in the class's mind about the subject of her essay. Then Haley took her seat.

Will passed Tig a note on a tiny scrap of paper. *She's kidding, right?*

Tig couldn't even look up from her desk. She knew her face was red, and she was afraid she might cry. She was so angry and frustrated. She shook her head. Will grabbed the paper and wrote something else, then tossed it back onto Tig's desk. *Don't let her get to you. She's a fake, and everybody knows it.*

If everybody knew it, though, why did they clap and cheer?

Chapter Twenty-Four

Claire had social studies a different period than the rest of the band, so she hadn't witnessed the theatrical production Haley had put on to destroy Tig.

Lunch was like a funeral visitation, Haley receiving visitors in the line and then at her table. The news of Haley's victimization had spread throughout the entire seventh grade, and girls eagerly awaited their turn to console the poor, persecuted martyr . . . all the while glaring at Tig. It wasn't that anyone actually believed Haley's story—they all knew what Haley was capable of and many of them had been on the receiving end of it at some point—but they played along because it was a chance to join in the drama while sucking up to the Bots.

"I think I'm going to throw up," Tig announced as she, Robbie, Olivia, Kyra, and Will watched the scene.

"Even the non-Bots want a piece of the action," Robbie said.

"Their grudges go viral fast," said Olivia.

"Yeah, hating Tig is about to become the cool new thing to do," Kyra said. "We've got trouble."

"So, thanks to Haley's 'anti-bullying' essay, everybody's going to start bullying Tig. Ironic, isn't it?" Will asked.

"Yes, but nobody will think of that," Tig said. "Man, this is ridiculous."

Just then Claire arrived at the lunch table. "What's going on over there?" she asked, taking her seat. "Did Haley have a death in her family or something? Is everything okay?"

"Haven't you heard?" Will said. "Tig murders puppies."

"What?" Claire looked confused.

"Haley's tragedy," Will continued. "It's all Tig's fault. Tig, you should be ashamed for being such a big, bad bully."

"Yeah," Robbie said. "Poor Haley will probably never recover. Oh, I feel so sorry for her. I know all this attention she's getting right now is tough on her, seeing as how she's so shy and all and doesn't enjoy people fawning over her."

"Tig," Claire asked, "what is all this about?"

Tig sighed. "Here's the deal . . . ," she began. "Haley used to be the lead singer for our band."

"For about five whole seconds," Robbie added. "Five screechy, horrible seconds."

"She wasn't a good singer; that's true," Tig replied. "But it wasn't just that. She was bossy and hard to work with. We ended up having to part ways."

"It wasn't Tig's fault," Olivia said. "She never asked her to be in the band in the first place. Kyra asked her."

"It seemed like a good idea at the time," Kyra said. "How was I supposed to know what would happen?"

"Okay," Claire said. "So why is it all of a sudden a big deal now? How long ago was this?"

"A couple of weeks ago," Tig said. "I thought it was water under the bridge. Guess not."

Will chimed in. "Today in social studies, Haley read an essay about how Tig had bullied her and hurt her feelings. Now Haley's got the sympathy vote and Tig's the bad guy."

"Were you mean to her?" Claire asked.

Tig looked down at her lunch bag. "Not at first," she said. "I mean, I tried not to be, but it sort of . . . escalated." It occurred to Tig that everything Haley and Regan had said to her that day in the gym had been said quietly. Tig was the one who'd raised her voice. To everyone else in the gym, it had probably looked like Tig was the crazy, mean one, and the Bots had done nothing to provoke her. Tig had to hand it to them: they were good at what they did.

"It was all Haley's fault," Robbie said. "Tig tried to be nice. But Haley was a real diva. She didn't leave Tig much choice. Heck, my grandma probably would've said worse to her than what Tig said."

"This is awkward," Claire said. "I mean, you guys are my friends, but Haley's my friend, too. I haven't told her about singing in the band. What if she feels like I've betrayed her?"

"Claire, don't you think it's a little strange that Haley never even knew you were alive until you started sitting at our lunch table?" said Robbie. "She's been plotting a way to get even with Tig—with all of us, really—since the day we kicked her out of the band."

"How can you be so sure?" Claire asked.

"Because that's how the Bots operate," Robbie said.

"I can't believe anyone would do something like that."

"No offense, Claire," Robbie said, "but you haven't been here very long. You haven't seen these girls in action."

"You're on our side, aren't you?" Olivia asked.

"I'm not on anyone's side," Claire replied. "I don't think it's right for me to take sides about an issue I wasn't involved in, when I don't really know what happened."

"You're not going to ditch us, are you?" Tig asked. "Although if you did, I guess I could understand. My name is going to be mud around here for a while until this dies down. You might not want to be associated with us."

"I'm not ditching anybody," said Claire. "I'll talk to Haley today in study hall. Who knows? Maybe this has all just been a big misunderstanding. Maybe I can negotiate a truce."

"And maybe this ridiculous dress I'm wearing will become a new fashion craze," Robbie said. "Good luck with that."

"But just in case," Claire said, "I may hold off on mentioning my involvement with the band."

"She's ditching us," Robbie said.

"I'm not!" Claire said. "But it seems imprudent to throw petrol on the fire at this point, don't you agree?"

"I agree," said Tig. "You do what you have to do, Claire. Thanks for not jumping to conclusions like"—Tig gestured toward the crowd surrounding Haley—"everyone else."

"Glad you're not jumping ship," Robbie said.

"Thanks for sticking with me, everybody," Tig said to her friends.

"Where else would I go, dressed like this?" Robbie said with a grin.

Tig tried not to let Claire's fair-mindedness feel like a betrayal. It wasn't. Her rational side told her that Claire was just being a good person, better than Tig would've been if the situation were reversed.

But her gut told her to get ready for losing the band's lead singer, and her cool new friend.

For the rest of the day, just navigating the hallways was a challenge for Tig. The Bots had missed their calling as military strategists. Their ability to flank Tig on every side while simultaneously running sneak attacks and setting up unbreachable lines was indeed impressive. Luckily, Robbie was with her when a minor Bot, a girl from the basketball team, ran right into Tig and knocked her backward.

"Hey!" Tig shouted. She was so taken by surprise, that was the best she could do.

"Hey what?" the basketball girl said. "You want to start something?"

"No," Tig said. "I was just—"

"You want to start something?" the basketball girl said again, backing Tig against the lockers.

Before Tig could respond, Robbie pushed Tig aside and stepped between her and the basketball girl. "*She* doesn't," Robbie said. "But maybe I do."

The basketball girl towered over Robbie, but Robbie didn't look the least bit scared. Tig marveled at her bravery. A small crowd had started to gather.

The basketball girl huffed. "What, do you know karate, you chink?" Someone called out, "Hey, not cool!"

"Call me a chink one more time and you'll find out." Robbie stared up at the girl without flinching. She looked so tough, so intimidating, even Tig shuddered.

The girl laughed, but Tig could tell it was forced. She was afraid. "*You're* going to fight *me*?"

"Here's what's going to happen," Robbie said. "You're going to walk away. Right now."

The girl just stood there. Robbie didn't flinch. "I said *now*."

"Whatever," the girl said. "I don't have time for this." She walked away.

When the crowd scattered, Tig stared in awe at Robbie.

"What?" Robbie asked.

"She's enormous!" Tig said, once she found her voice again. "And you weren't even scared. Not even a little bit! Would you really have fought her? And, hey, I'm sorry about the name-calling."

"Ripley, it's all about attitude. A good bluff is worth a multitude of punches. Act like you can kick their butts, and they'll think you just might be able to. And you know there are jerks everywhere. Come on. Let's get to class."

As they walked together, Tig wondered if anyone else on the planet could ever be as cool as Robbie Chan.

Chapter Twenty-Five

That Friday night, Tig stayed over at Kyra's. With what Tig had endured at school since Haley's outing her as "the bully," the idea of an evening with Aunt Laurie felt like a cakewalk.

Another reason Tig couldn't refuse the sleepover invitation? Kyra had promised to share a secret. A secret so big, she promised, it would change Tig's destiny. Right about now a change of destiny sounded pretty good to Tig.

Kyra had been reserved and fearful the rest of Monday after Haley'd read her essay, and she was even more skittish on Tuesday. But by Wednesday, Kyra had been practically giddy. "There's nothing to worry about!" she'd told Tig and the other girls. "I've got this one all figured out!" Whenever Tig tried to get anything out of her, Kyra would promise that the big secret, which she would reveal only when the moment was right, would change everything. Given Kyra's recent history with inviting Haley to sing in the band, Tig was more than a little anxiety-ridden.

Kyra had made Tig wait through supper, with no hint of the plan or whatever it was she'd come up with to fix Tig's problems.

It wasn't until they went to change into their pajamas for the night that Kyra was ready to talk. "Who has the best cousin ever?" she asked as she pulled her bra through the arm of her sweatshirt and tossed it onto the bed. It was a cup size too large. Kyra had bought it that way on purpose. Her plan was to grow bigger boobs based on the power of positive thinking. So far, it hadn't worked, but Kyra hadn't given up yet.

"I don't know," Tig replied. "I'm going to need

more information before I answer that question."

Kyra threw Tig a pair of sweatpants from her dresser drawer. "Then information you shall have." She took her laptop off the desk and sat on the beanbag chair, leaving room for Tig to join her. She typed in a Web address and said, "Take a look at this!"

It was an Evite.

To Kyra's birthday party in two weeks.

And the big headline said, *Featuring, Live in Concert, Pandora's Box.*

Tig's stomach dropped. "What have you done?!"

"Are you surprised? I sent it out to everyone when you got here. I made sure not to send it to you, of course, because I wanted to see the look on your face."

Tig asked again, "What have you done?!"

"What do you mean what have I done? I've saved your reputation! Haley's been telling everyone you're a loser. So all we have to do to thwart her is show everyone you're not a loser! You're cool, and you're in an awesome rock band!"

"But, Kyra . . . I'm not in an awesome rock band!

I'm in a beginner band, and we stink!"

"No, we don't! We were great at your aunt Kate's party!"

Tig stood up. She was about to lose it. "Kyra! Are you out of your mind? That was *one* song! That does not a concert make!"

"Well, we almost know 'Plush,' and we know Claire sings that great."

"Wow, two whole songs! And that's assuming we get 'Plush' fine-tuned in two weeks. And, as I recall, you were pretty lost on the intro to that song."

"I'll have it by the party."

"Just for the sake of argument, let's say you do. Then guess what? We will have two songs! Whoopee! Kyra, two songs is not a set list! We will be laughed off the stage!"

"The problem with you is, you don't believe in positive thinking."

"The problem with you is, you don't believe in . . . reality!"

"Can't you just *try* to have a positive outlook?"

"Sure. Two weeks from now we're going to be rock goddesses." Tig picked up Kyra's bra off the bed and threw it at her. "And you'll have giant boobs." Tig started digging around in her bag. "Where is my phone? I've got to call Robbie."

"Robbie this, Robbie that," Kyra whined. "I bet you wish Robbie was your cousin instead of me."

"Oh, don't try to change the subject. I'm calling Robbie and, meanwhile, you're going to take down the Evite . . . or cancel it . . . or . . . How many people did you invite, anyway?"

"I don't know . . . only, like, fifty or so people."

"Fifty people?!"

"My mom's letting me have my party at that gorgeous new pavilion on the river."

"Of course she is."

"What's that supposed to mean?"

It meant that Kyra's mom was spending a fortune to throw an ostentatious party, but Tig knew better than to veer into family insults. "It means cancel the band! Take it down!" As Tig ranted, her phone rang.

"It's Robbie."

"Naturally."

Tig rolled her eyes and answered the phone. "Hey."

"Have you seen this Evite?" Robbie was uncharacteristically shrill.

"Yes, I have. You don't have to say anything. She's taking it down right now."

"No, I'm not!" Kyra said.

"Yes, you are!"

"Well, I hope she is," Robbie said. "We're barely solid on one song!"

"Tell me about it. Kyra says she'll learn 'Plush' by then."

"No way," Robbie said. "Those chromatic riffs in the intro are too hard for a beginner bass player. I was probably overly optimistic to even suggest that song for us at this point."

"Positive thinking abounds all around me," Tig said.

"There's no way we can play her party."

"I know. It would be an absolute disaster," agreed Tig.

"Maybe for you," Robbie said. "I won't even be in

town that weekend. It's my great-grandma's eightieth birthday. In Florida."

Tig relayed the info to Kyra and then said, "Imagine how those two songs will sound without a guitar player."

"We could get someone else to fill in," Kyra said.

"No," Tig said, covering the phone with her other hand. "Absolutely not. First of all, we're not doing this, and second of all, Robbie is part of Pandora's Box, and we don't play without her." She spoke into the phone again. "Don't worry about a thing. We'll handle it."

When Tig was off the phone, she took the laptop from Kyra. "How many people have responded?"

"Twenty-six at my last count," Kyra said.

Tig scanned the list. "You invited Edgy Abz?" Tig asked. "Why would you invite her?"

"Who's that?"

"The redheaded rapper. From the audition?"

"I didn't invite her," Kyra said. "What are you talking about?"

Tig looked at the names of all the people who'd

said they were attending. She didn't recognize more than six or seven people from their school. "Who are these people?"

"I don't know," Kyra said. "I didn't invite them."

"Oh no. Kyra, somebody hacked into the invitation and sent the Evite out to strangers. What admin password did you use?"

" 'Kyra,' " she said.

"Wow, who could crack that code?" Tig said. "Passwords are supposed to be secure, Kyra!"

"It's just an Evite!" Kyra said. "I didn't think it was a government secret!"

Tig began looking up the names of the attendees on Facebook. One, two, three . . . eight . . . twelve . . . "They all go to County."

County Middle School was Lakeview Heights's football rival. There was intense scorn on both sides.

"Who would invite County people?" Kyra said.

"Did you invite Haley?" Tig responded.

"Well, yeah," Kyra said. "And Regan and Sofia, too. I thought, you know, it might be a nice peace gesture.

CHAPTER TWENTY-FIVE

Plus, Mom told me to."

"Kyra, don't you get it? Regan must know somebody at County who she sent the info to and then she told them to spread it around. That's how Edgy Abz saw it. Don't you remember what she said at the audition? She said she'd be there when we gigged so she could burn us to the ground."

"Oh, I'd forgotten about that."

"We'd be walking into an ambush. Edgy Abz will get all her friends from County to come and heckle us. Cancel it," Tig said. "Now."

"I can't cancel the party!"

"Then cancel the part about the band."

"Okay, okay," Kyra said. She edited the invitation. "Are you happy now?"

"I'm deliriously overjoyed."

But even with the change made, Tig couldn't sleep that night. What could Kyra possibly have been thinking?

Regan was behind the leak to County; Tig knew it. She also had to have been behind the essay. Haley was too dense to come up with plans on her own.

The question was, exactly what did Regan hope to accomplish by inviting County kids to the party? How could she have known about Edgy Abz's beef with Pandora's Box? But with social media, everyone knew everything. Especially since people like Edgy Abz were likely to keep their profiles public and post everything that made them mad. Tig couldn't resist. She looked up Edgy Abz's profile on her phone. It was wide open, no privacy settings. And there it was. The post.

It's goin' down at this party. Lakeview girls who dissed my rhymes about to get schooled. You gotta be there to see it. #revenge #lightthefuse #pumped.

Then she linked to the Evite.

Tig's stomach tied itself in a knot. What a trap they would've walked into! Thank goodness, she'd gotten Kyra to cancel the performance.

But now that the plan for County kids to heckle them at Kyra's party had been ruined, what would the Bots come up with for plan B?

Chapter Twenty-Six

On the upside, people at school started talking to Tig again.

On the downside, all they wanted to talk about was the band. How long had they had a band? What kind of music did they play? Who was in it? And, of course, why had they canceled on Kyra's party?

Tig realized that the idea of having a band was a lot easier than the reality. It seemed that everyone at school looked at her differently . . . sort of with admiration and interest.

But despite the temptation to exaggerate (how she

wanted to say something like, *Yeah, we've only got about twenty-nine songs on the set list so far* or *I'm working on some original music so we can lock up a recording contract*), Tig downplayed the whole thing. Of course, she didn't feel the need to overshare either. When asked why the gig had been canceled, she simply replied, "Our guitarist is going to be out of town." Which, of course, was true. She just omitted *And we know only one song, and sometimes Kyra and I even flub that one.*

After all, some things were better left unsaid.

That was what Tig thought.

Haley did not, however, share that opinion.

Before the bell rang in math class and the teacher was out policing the halls, Justin Watkins, a second-stringer on the football team, started in on Tig. "Haley tells me your band stinks."

Tig felt her face go red, but she tried to keep her cool. "Oh, she does, does she?"

"Yeah," Justin continued. "She said y'all aren't even a real band and that you don't even have a lead singer because she quit."

"Haley's saying she quit our band?"

"Yeah. Said she quit because the band stinks so bad."

"So last week the story was that I bullied her out of the band, and this week the story is that she quit. Do you see the inconsistency, Justin?"

Justin looked confused.

Tig continued. "How could I have kicked her out of the band if she quit?"

Logic, however, was lost on Justin and, apparently, the rest of the student body. It was like a bad soap opera where the writers forget the previous week's storylines when they write new scripts. The fickle middle-school public didn't care that Haley's stories contradicted each other; the truth was much less intriguing than the stories the Bots told.

Tig cursed herself for forgetting to pack a drink that day. She had no choice but to get in the lunch line to buy a carton of milk. The Bots were way ahead of her, but upon seeing her, they ditched their spot to join her at the line's end.

"How humiliating about your band," Regan said.

"There's nothing humiliating about my band," Tig said. She looked at Haley. "At least not anymore." There was a twitter of *ooh*s from the audience.

"There must be," Regan continued, "if you're afraid to play Kyra's party."

"We're not afraid of anything. Our guitarist is going to be out of town."

"And I guess there's only one person in town who knows how to play a guitar," said Regan.

"There's only one guitarist in our band. It's called loyalty."

"Or an excuse," Regan replied.

"I wouldn't even think about playing a gig unless every member of the band could make it. It's what real bands do, out of respect for the audience. They come to see Pandora's Box, not mostly Pandora's Box and subs. But you wouldn't know anything about the music business." Tig was pretty pleased with herself. She actually didn't have the first clue as to whether real bands ever subbed musicians, but she thought throwing around the "music business" stuff made her sound like she knew what she was talking about and might be enough to shut Regan up.

"You are such a loser," said Regan. "Say whatever you want, but we all know you're just afraid to show everyone you're not really in a *real* band. Everybody knows you're a poser, pretending to be cool when you're not."

"Yeah, if you were really a good band, you'd play," said some guy from behind them in line.

"I'd play in a heartbeat if I had a band," said a random girl in the line. "What's the big deal?"

"Anybody can say they're in a band," said another guy. "Why doesn't she just prove it?"

There was a lot of muttering. It seemed the whole lunch line had an opinion about Tig and her band. "This is *so* not your business!" Tig said loudly enough for the whole line to hear. But no one stopped muttering. It was like they'd all made up their minds about Tig and Pandora's Box, and there was nothing she could do to change that.

Tig couldn't stand it. "Listen, everybody," Tig said even more loudly this time. "If I thought for one second I could find a guitarist on such short notice, I'd show you all who's in a 'real' band!"

"I play a little guitar."

Tig froze. The voice sounded just like Will's.

She turned around. It was Will.

"You play drums," Tig said. "Not guitar."

"I prefer drums," Will said. "But I dabble with guitar. I mean, I'm not great or anything, but I just heard something about you needing a guitarist. Maybe I could help?"

Tig wanted to die. Where were freak medical anomalies like teenage aneurysms when she needed one? "No offense, Will, but I mean, our guitarist is pretty advanced."

"See? She's chicken," said Regan. "What's the matter, Tig? The nerd prince has come to your rescue, so now you have no excuse. Are you going to put up or shut up? Either your 'band' plays at Kyra's party or you admit you can't really play at all."

"Oh, wait . . . ," Will began. "I didn't know what y'all were talking about. I just caught the last part and I thought—" No one was listening.

"She won't do it," said Haley. "I'm telling you, they stink."

"Oh, we'll play, all right," Tig said. "And then we'll just see who stinks."

"Great," said Regan. "I know I can't wait."

"Me neither," said Tig.

As the Bots paid for their bottled water and salads, Tig's head began to throb. She paid for her milk and sat down next to Olivia at their table.

"What's wrong?" Robbie asked.

"Nothing," said Tig. "Except that I just made a huge, horrible mistake."

Chapter Twenty-Seven

"**A**nd that, kiddos, is a little thing the Greeks liked to call 'hubris.'" Leave it to Robbie to have an intellectual take on Tig's complete screwup.

"I know," Tig said. "I don't know what got into me. I can't believe I got pulled into their smack talk. They totally set me up. They knew I wouldn't be able to back down and that my big mouth would get me in trouble."

"Get *you* in trouble?" Claire said. "Tig, I don't know if I can do this! You know I have terrible stage fright! You said we were going to ease me into this lead singer business."

"You were great at my aunt's party," Tig said.

"But you never said anything about getting up in front of all our classmates in a mere two weeks!"

"It's not you I'm worried about, Claire," said Tig. "I know you don't know it, but you could rock Madison Square Garden if you felt like it. I'm worried about the rest of the band."

"You knew I'd be in Florida," said Robbie.

"I know," Tig said again. "It's like I told you, I let them trap me. I couldn't back down. Are you mad?"

"Kinda," Robbie said. "But I'll get over it."

"Robbie, please don't be mad," Tig said. "I would never purposely not want you to play with us. You know that."

"I do know that," Robbie said. "You shot your mouth off. Been there. I'd probably be more upset if I thought you could actually pull this off without me. I mean, not to sound arrogant, but you kind of need me."

"We *totally* need you!" Tig said. "I don't know what we're going to do."

"I can do it," Olivia said. "I'm in town that weekend."

"I'm not worried about you either," said Tig. "You can play anything. You've been at this a little longer than Kyra and I have."

"So we'll learn a few songs!" Kyra said. "Pick some easy ones. We can do it! Hey, most rock stars are on tons of dope all the time, right? If they can play stoned, I'm sure we can play sober."

"Kyra, we can barely play at all!" Tig reminded her. "Unless you've suddenly mastered those fills with the sixteenth notes on 'Plush' and just forgotten to tell me." Then she turned on Will. "And you! Why'd you have to butt in, Mr. Helpful?"

Will looked hurt.

"It's not Will's fault," Olivia said.

Tig shook her head. "You're right. Sorry, Will. You were just trying to help. Totally not your fault."

"I thought the whole point of starting this band was that it was supposed to be an *all-girl* band," said Robbie.

"That was the original idea," Tig said. "And that's what I still want, ultimately."

"Looks like you're going to have to make an exception. At least for one performance," Robbie said. "So, Will, how good are you on the guitar?"

"Just barely decent," Will replied. "The only song I know the whole way through is that One Nothing song, 'Gotcha.'"

"I *love* that song!" Claire said. "Their lead singer is brilliant!"

"I may or may not have had a huge crush on her at some point," Will said. "She's so cool. And so beautiful."

Huh. That was interesting. Will had told Tig once that he thought she looked like the lead singer of One Nothing. But she didn't know at the time that Will thought the singer was beautiful.

"Yes, she is," said Robbie. "Good voice. Not quite as growly as somebody else I know, though."

"Oh my gosh!" Kyra said. "Claire, your voice would be *perfect* on that song!"

"Think you could learn it in time for the party, Ripley?" Robbie asked.

"I don't know," Tig said. "That song's pretty fast."

"That's true," Robbie said. "But then again, you always play everything too fast anyway."

"You've got a point," Tig said. Whenever she got excited about getting the coordination down, she always played faster. "I don't know. I'd have to look at it."

"Will, you're sure you can handle that song on guitar?" asked Robbie.

"I'm not sure. I used to be able to do it pretty well, but it's been a while since I practiced. I guess I could get it all down again in a couple of weeks if I practiced every day."

"I could help you," Robbie said. "And Olivia's golden with the keyboard. Get her the sheet music, and she can play anything. Claire, what do you think?"

"I don't know," she said. "I do love that song, but . . ."

"You can do it," Robbie said. "So, really, it depends on Kyra and Tig."

"What if we said yes?" Tig said. "We still don't have a set. That's just one song."

"So you play just one song," Robbie said. "Tell them that because your regular guitarist is out of town, this is just a preview. And don't, under any circumstances, admit that this is the only song you guys can play! One song played well would shut them up. If you can pull it off. Can you?"

They all looked at Kyra and Tig.

Then the two of them looked at each other.

Tig could feel the hopefulness of everyone else at the table. She didn't want to be the one to ruin it. "Positive thinking?" she said to Kyra.

Kyra responded with an enthusiastic hug.

"So I guess we're all in," Tig said.

"I'll try," Claire said. "But honestly, I can't make any promises."

"She's in," Robbie said. "Just blindfold her so she can't see the audience. She'll nail it."

"It's not just that," Claire said. "I don't know—I mean, I still hardly know anyone here, and now I'm supposed to sing in front of a bunch of strangers? I already told you that I like singing, but I don't feel comfortable *performing*. I'm not sure I'm cut out to front a rock band. Maybe it's not my thing."

Tig wondered if Haley had been talking to Claire about not being lumped in with Tig's crowd. She wanted to ask but dared not.

"So make it your thing," Robbie said. "At least give it a try."

"I suppose it can't hurt," Claire said, but she didn't sound thrilled.

"Wish I could be there to throw it in Regan's face," Robbie said. "But you guys will have to throw it in her face without me."

As Tig picked over her turkey sandwich, she thought of a quote she'd learned in social studies:

"Eat, drink, and be merry . . . for tomorrow we die."

In her mind, she changed *tomorrow* to *in two weeks*.

Chapter Twenty-Eight

Lee was, to say the least, dubious about Tig's new project.

"That's not an easy song," Lee said. "You might want to get a little more experience under your belt before you try to tackle something that ambitious."

"I kind of don't have a choice," Tig said. "It's the only song my substitute guitarist knows, and to be honest, I'm trying to win over my lead singer. She's so awesome, and I'm afraid she's going to leave us if I don't give her a song she can't resist."

Lee made a face that was at once both a smile and

a grimace. "You certainly are learning pretty quickly what it's like to have a band."

Tig felt a little relieved to know that all bands— even ones that weren't led by a novice—had similar problems. "So, can you teach it to me?"

"I can try," Lee said.

Band practice was set for four o'clock daily at Tig's house, except for weekends, when they'd try to get together after lunch and work as long as possible. On this particular weekday afternoon, however, Robbie had taken the day to work on her science project, since she wasn't playing the party.

"Maybe we should've picked a different song," Tig said. "This open and closed hi-hat groove during the bridge is really hard. Not to mention some of these drum fills during the chorus and at the end of the breakdown."

"Why can't we just play 'Sweet Home'?" Kyra asked.

"Because Will doesn't know that one," Tig said. "He said it took him all summer to learn the One Nothing song, so we're lucky he knows this one. Guitar isn't his thing. No offense, Will."

"None taken."

"It's really sweet of you to help us out like this, Will," said Olivia.

"No prob." Will hardly looked up from his guitar. He was fiddling with the knobs at the end, tightening the strings or something; Tig wasn't sure what.

"We really do owe you," Tig added.

Will looked up at her and grinned. "I'll collect one of these days."

"Let's run through it again from the top," Tig said.

Kyra let out a whine. "I'm tired!"

Tig gritted her teeth. This was just like Kyra—all bouncing off the walls with enthusiasm one minute, and then losing interest as soon as the initial excitement waned. "Get un-tired," Tig said.

"I'm feeling a bit winded myself," Claire said. Tig had noticed that Claire hadn't said much all during practice. She seemed distant.

"It's almost time to go," Will said.

"We need longer practices if we're going to get this right," Tig replied.

"Sorry, slave driver. A boy's got to do his homework. You finish that science project yet?"

"Almost." Tig was embarrassed to admit she hadn't even started. It was the big nine-weeks project that had been assigned at the beginning of the term, an exploration that involved the five steps of the scientific method, complete with research and a technical report, photographs of the student involved in the exploration, and an interactive computer demonstration to present to the class. It wasn't exactly a project one could scribble out the period before it was due. Tig should have started on it weeks ago, but she'd thought she had plenty of time. And she would have, if it hadn't been for the performance at Kyra's party coming at her out of nowhere.

"What's your topic?" Will asked.

"No time to discuss science," Tig said before leading the count-off.

The song they played sounded not at all like the

One Nothing song, or even a song at all. More like a bunch of instruments clanging on top of one another. Tig hoped it was just the acoustics in the studio, or how loud the drums sounded from her vantage point, or that the cymbals that had come with her reasonably priced drum kit were cheap and awful (good cymbals had to be bought separately and cost more than a hundred dollars apiece). But Tig doubted that cymbal quality or acoustics were the band's real problem.

They were able to run through the song only once more before five o'clock came, along with the band's mothers and their minivans.

"One hour a day isn't going to cut it," Tig told Will. "We are going to look like complete losers."

"Pretty much," Will agreed.

Tig studied Will a moment. "So why are you doing this?" she asked. "This isn't your problem. Don't you care that you're going to be completely humiliated? What in the world would possess you to jump on board the *Titanic* with us?"

Will laughed. "Well, it's not like I have such a cool

reputation to protect."

Olivia had just finished packing up her keyboard. "Will, you're the best."

"Hey, when you're right, you're right," he said. Tig half expected cartoon stars and hearts to dance around Olivia's face as she gazed at Will.

Once everyone had gone home, Tig should have gone inside to work on her science project. And her worksheet for English. And her homework pages for math.

But she stayed with her drums until her mom called her in for supper.

Chapter Twenty-Nine

The Tuesday before the party, Claire was absent at school.

Tig tried not to panic, but her mind immediately jumped to catastrophe mode. What if Claire was sick?

She'd seemed a bit run-down at practice over the weekend, and even more so on Monday. Claire had still sung great, but she'd looked pale (even for her alabaster complexion) and had had to sit down between run-throughs.

Tig sneaked her phone out in the bathroom stall between first and second period and texted, *U okay?*

Where R U?

Doc office, Claire replied.

???

Don't know yet.

Tig grabbed Kyra's arm in the hallway. "This is bad, this is bad, this is bad."

"What?" Kyra said. "What's wrong with you? Are you all right?"

"Maybe," Tig replied. "Maybe I'm all right. For now. But Claire isn't."

"What do you mean?"

"I mean Claire is, right this very minute, at the doctor's office. She's sick."

"I'm sure she'll live," Kyra said. "Don't be so melodramatic."

Tig couldn't believe her cousin. "Yes, I'm sure it's not life-threatening, but need I remind you that your party is in three days? And that we have to play this party and sound at least halfway decent? We need Claire for that. Without Claire, we're sunk!"

"Don't get yourself all worked up. She's probably

fine."

Maybe Kyra was right. Tig wanted her to be right. No, she *needed* her to be right.

But she doubted it.

Something inside told Tig that the gig situation was about to go from bad to worse.

As soon as school was out for the day and she could check her phone again, Tig found a text from Claire waiting for her:

Mono.

Needless to say, Claire wouldn't make practice that day. Or any day before Kyra's party.

Robbie had skipped many of the practices lately since a) she wasn't playing the gig and b) she was so far ahead of Tig and Kyra in skill that they needed about half a dozen practices to catch up with her anyway. But since she would be leaving on Thursday for her great-grandmother's party, she'd come to offer whatever help she could before she went out of town and left Tig and the others to falter.

"Maybe she'll be well by Friday," Kyra offered.

"It's mono," Tig said, burying her face in her hands. "Mono hangs on for, like, ever."

"Or at least long enough to keep her from singing at the gig," Robbie said. "You don't suppose Claire got sick—you know, conveniently—so she would have an excuse not to perform at the party?"

"Of course not," Tig said. "Claire wouldn't do that. Besides, you saw her these past few days. She's looked like microwaved death on a plate."

"I'm just saying, her timing certainly is perfect if she doesn't want Regan and Haley to know she's in our band."

"Maybe we should all get mono," Tig said. "And with any luck, I'll die a quick death from mine."

"If you catch it, let me know," Will said. "Maybe you can give it to me."

"You're just going to have to cancel," Robbie said. "Musicians cancel shows all the time for illnesses and whatnot. It happens. Like, remember a couple of years ago when Rod Stewart was supposed to play the amphitheater? My mom and all her friends had tickets, and then he canceled because he needed 'vocal rest' or something. But they all understood and everybody moved on."

"Yeah, but nobody went around saying that Rod Stewart canceled because he can't really sing," Tig said. "That was one show out of a zillion. He's proven himself for decades. This is our first performance."

"Technically, it isn't Pandora's Box's first performance," Robbie said. "Your aunt's party was."

"But that was just for old people," Tig replied. "Nobody our age saw us. It might as well have not even happened. We can't cancel. We have to show Regan we're a real band."

"Well, if you're not going to cancel," Robbie said, "one of you jokers has got to sing lead."

They all looked at one another.

"Tell you what," Tig said. "Let's run through once without vocals; then we'll make a decision." Tig wanted to benefit from Robbie's help with the music before she worried about the singing.

They ran through the song once. When she could

look up from what she was playing, Tig watched Robbie. The look on her face was a mixture of pity and pain.

"Is it as bad as I thought?" Tig asked when they were finished with the song.

"Only if you thought it was, like, bubonic plague bad," Robbie said.

Tig cringed. "I was afraid of that. I've been telling myself it's because I can't hear it right because I'm back behind the drums."

"Kyra, you've got to pick up some momentum on the chorus," Robbie said. "And, Tig, you're dragging, too. Will, let me show you a couple of things with the intro. You've got to stick it pretty hard there if you want to give the song the energy it needs."

While Robbie worked with Will, Tig and Kyra worked on the bass and drums together. Then they ran through once more all together, but it wasn't much better.

"Not much else you can do at this point but keep trying," Robbie said. "If you can lay some strong vocals over it, that might help. Who's game?"

Robbie "auditioned" all three girls by making them sing the lead a cappella. Olivia was too soprano; Kyra hit too many wrong notes; and Tig was passable but lacked the force and volume to really carry it.

"Will, let's hear you," Robbie said.

"Huh?"

"Let's hear you on the vocals," Robbie repeated. "Whatcha got?"

"Oh, no way," Will said. "It's all I can do to play the right notes on the guitar. I can't do that and sing at the same time."

"Will's doing more than we should ask of him already," Tig said.

"Thanks, Tig," Will said.

"Besides, I've heard you sing, and you're not that good."

"Ouch!"

"Just saying . . . fifth-grade graduation when we sang 'Climb Every Mountain'? It wasn't pretty."

"I can live with that," said Will.

"Tig, it's up to you, then," Robbie said.

"Fine," Tig said. "Mic me."

Robbie set the audio up so Tig's voice rang out over the drums.

"Telling anyone who will listen . . ." Tig sang.

The song was hard enough to play anyway, but now that Tig had to concentrate on the lyrics as well, it was more than she could handle. The song sounded even worse than before.

When it was time for everyone to go, Tig was almost glad. She knew they needed more time, but she was mentally exhausted and overwhelmed.

Oh, she'd keep practicing, all right. But she wanted time to practice alone, with no one to look at her when she messed up.

"I can't practice tomorrow," Will said. "I've got to finish that project for science, and Mom says I can't leave the house for any reason until it's done."

"No problem," Tig said. "We've done all we can do at this point anyway. I'll practice alone and see if I can improve on my end. Kyra, you'll do the same." It wasn't a request; it was a command.

"Will, you're sure you don't know 'Sweet Home Alabama'?" Robbie asked.

"I wish I did," said Will.

"It's fine," Tig said. "We'll make it work. One song. It's not the end of the world."

Tig stayed in the studio until supper, then returned and stayed until bedtime.

She still hadn't started on her science project, but she was going to nail the chorus at least, even if it killed her.

Chapter Thirty

Friday morning Tig gave serious consideration to the idea of faking sick.

Not only was she exhausted, she still hadn't perfected the song for the party. If she stayed home, she could work on it the whole day.

Plus, she could avoid having to tell Mr. Ellis that she didn't have her science project. She might get lucky, and Mr. Ellis would be too busy to call her mom until the beginning of next week—after the party was over.

But one thing stopped her.

Tig knew that if she were too sick for school, her mom would say she was too sick for Kyra's party, and although part of her desperately wished her mom would forbid her to go, she knew that if she didn't show, Regan would never let her hear the end of how she'd chickened out.

Tig had to show up at the party that night, and she had to play drums.

Oh, and sing lead. Who could forget that?

Tig muttered curses upon the universe as she thought of it all.

She tried to make herself small in science class that day so that maybe Mr. Ellis wouldn't notice her. As the class went in alphabetical order to present their projects, many of them took so long, Tig thought maybe they wouldn't get to the *R*s at all. Then on Monday she could quietly slip her display board onto the back lab tables with the others, and no one would be the wiser. She was so busy thinking about how great that would be, Mr. Ellis had to call her name twice before she heard him. "Ripley, you're up!"

The class turned and looked at her.

Mr. Ellis looked at her. "Ripley?"

Tig said nothing, just shook her head.

"Really?" Mr. Ellis asked.

Tig nodded.

"Okay, then. Roberts."

When the period was over, Tig tried to exit without Mr. Ellis's catching her. "Not so fast, Ripley."

She turned and walked back to him as though he were the executioner. "I'm sorry, Mr. Ellis."

"Are you?" Mr. Ellis said. "I'm not sure you realize quite how sorry you need to be. Tig, this is a big deal. This is your nine-weeks' project."

"I know. Can I bring it in on Monday?"

"How far along are you?"

Tig wanted to lie. She wanted to say she was almost finished. But she liked Mr. Ellis; everyone did. "I'm ashamed to tell you."

"Tig, this isn't like you. Is everything okay?"

"No, sir."

"How can I help?"

"You could not call my folks," Tig said with a weak smile.

"Have we met?" Mr. Ellis said. "I'm Mr. Ellis. I'm the call-your-parents-when-I'm-concerned guy. Besides, if you're having trouble, your parents and I want to work with you to help you."

"I know," Tig said. "I'll turn it in Monday, I promise."

"See that you do. If I don't get your project Monday, your parents will be getting a call. Fair enough?"

"Thanks, Mr. Ellis."

Tig promised herself she'd do something spectacular after the party and turn it in Monday. A late grade would be better than a zero.

But she couldn't think about that now. One thing at a time. Her first order of business would be getting through the performance that night.

As she left Mr. Ellis's room, she ran straight into the Bots.

"Well, if it isn't Rihanna," Regan said.

Tig didn't even bother trying to tell her that she

was a drummer, not a singer. Because really, there was no reason trying to clarify an insult, and oh yeah, Tig was having to sing after all. So Tig said nothing.

"What, no comeback? Where's the smack talk you're so famous for? Or are you less cocky now that the big day has come?"

"I'm tired," Tig said. "Too tired to bother with you."

"No big," Regan said. "There's nothing you can say anyway. Your performance at the party tonight will do all the talking for you, won't it?"

"I guess so," Tig said. She had no more fight left in her.

Chapter Thirty-One

Aunt Laurie didn't like the idea of Pandora's Box playing at Kyra's party. Not one bit.

Finally something Tig and Aunt Laurie could agree on.

"Kyra, are you *sure* about this?" Aunt Laurie asked for the fifth time as the band set up their instruments before the party.

"We just need to get it over with," Kyra said. Even Kyra couldn't pretend any longer that everything was going to be okay.

"Want to run through?" Will asked.

"No," Tig said. She was sick of the whole thing. She'd practiced nonstop for days now and didn't want to be reminded of how bad they sounded all together. "Just give me some time to practice alone." When everyone else went to the pavilion's kitchen area to help Aunt Laurie check on the food, Tig gave it one last try. She was still rough on the chorus, but maybe if she just kept going instead of trying to go back and fix what she'd messed up, no one would notice.

Will came back into the party room alone. "It's going to be all right, you know."

"How?" Tig said. "How is any of this going to be all right?"

"It's not like anyone's going to die."

"Death before dishonor?" Tig placed her sticks on the snare. "The crowd is going to eat us alive."

"On the upside, I'm probably delicious," Will said. "Nice and tender."

Tig was too tired, too annoyed, and too worried to even think about laughing. Nothing was going to make her feel any better until this night was over. She almost didn't care anymore if they crashed and burned. At least the agony of dreading it would end.

Olivia came in. "Tig, we've at least got to do a sound check before the party starts."

Tig agreed. Olivia called Kyra in, and they played the song once through. "Kyra, have you been practicing at all?" Tig asked.

"Um, some of us had science projects to do!" Kyra threw back at her.

"You're the one who started this whole thing in the first place!" Tig said. But deep down, Tig knew she had only herself to blame. Yes, it was Kyra's stupid idea, but she had canceled the performance immediately after Tig had asked her to. Tig knew that, ultimately, it was her own pride—and her own big mouth—that had put her and the band in this position. "You know what?" Tig said. "Forget it."

She walked off the stage.

"Tig, you want to try it once more?" Will called.

The heavy doors slammed shut behind her.

Chapter Thirty-Two

Aunt Laurie must've spent a fortune on the party. Tig wondered how she would top it when the time came for Kyra's sweet sixteen. There was so much food—shrimp, roast beef, fruit, a chocolate fountain, and all manner of sweets. It seemed a shame to waste it on a bunch of middle-school kids who would've been perfectly happy with a few pizzas.

It seemed a bigger shame to waste so much of it on middle-school kids Kyra didn't even know.

Amid Kyra's friends from school and youth group, the club's main room was also packed with County kids who Tig and Kyra had never met. Well, except for Edgy Abz.

Kyra was having a meltdown. "Why are all these random strangers at my party?"

Will handed Tig his iPhone. "This might clear things up."

It was Regan's Twitter feed. She'd hashtagged County Middle School and written, *Big party! Everyone invited!*

"And Regan's probably intimidated almost everyone from school," Tig told her. "A lot of people you invited won't be showing." In a way, she was glad. Maybe Regan had done her a favor without meaning to. At least fewer people from school would see them play. Tig handed Will's phone to Kyra.

"Why would she do this?" Kyra said.

"Why do you think? Or have you forgotten they have it in for us?"

"Well, I didn't do anything! You're the one who told them off, not me! All I've ever tried to do is be nice to them!"

"No, you didn't do anything, Kyra," Tig said. "Except

invite Haley to be our lead singer in the first place, thus forcing me to kick her out. And advertising that we'd play at your stupid party so we could look like idiots."

"My party is not stupid!"

Before Tig could say anything back, Edgy Abz began shouting, "Where's the band?" and several County boys whooped their agreement. Soon the crowd of strangers was shouting, *"Band! Band! Band!"*

"Looks like it's do-or-die time," Tig said to Will.

"I hope we do," Will said.

The band took the stage and settled in with their instruments. Tig spoke into the mic. "Our guitarist is out of town and our lead singer is sick, so we're just going to do one song tonight. Here goes." She counted off with her sticks.

Tig didn't fall apart all at once. She was able to keep it together for the first few seconds of the song. The thought crossed Tig's mind that they might actually pull this thing off.

But when the chorus began, everything went crazy.

Tig and Kyra got way out of sync, and Tig couldn't

hear Will anymore. The fill going into the chorus tripped her up, and Tig started dragging on the rhythm. Kyra couldn't stay in the pocket. Tig couldn't stop singing the lyrics so that she could pick back up with the proper count.

The crowd began booing and heckling. Tig could see that several guys in the audience were holding up their arms and giving thumbs-down. She could also see that several others were holding up their phones, recording the car wreck that was happening before their eyes. Tig tried to recover a few times, but it was all a complete mess. Finally she was so scattered, she couldn't even remember the words to the song anymore, so she just stopped. So did Kyra. Then Will and Olivia stopped too.

"Fail!" Edgy Abz yelled. "Play something! Play something now!"

Tig recalled how she'd insisted to Regan that Pandora's Box would play at Kyra's party. She had no choice; she had to play something. Panicked, Tig started pounding out the backbeat of "Sweet Home," but Will didn't know that song, and without a guitar, no one else knew what to do, so Tig stopped. Now, panicked even more, she started on "Plush," but got through only the first couple of measures and the ruff before remembering that Will didn't know that song either, and Kyra had never mastered it. Olivia was staring at her in complete confusion. *What do you want me to do?* Olivia's eyes seemed to say.

Finally Tig threw her sticks onto the ground and walked off the stage and into the crowd, pushing past the cameras flashing in her face.

She knew it was wrong, as the leader, to leave her bandmates up onstage like that, with no hint of what to do. Like a captain going down with his sinking ship, she should have stood with her band and stoically endured the booing. She shouldn't have walked away. But she didn't care. She kept walking.

Just as she opened the doors, Edgy Abz shouted, "Pandora's Box in the house!" to which the crowd laughed uproariously.

Before even ten minutes had passed, the entire debacle was posted on YouTube.

Chapter Thirty-Three

Tig refused to get out of bed on Saturday.

She'd gone straight to her room when she'd gotten home from Kyra's party. She'd turned her phone on silent, and although she could hear the frequent *Errrrr* of a text or call coming in, she refused to even look at the screen to see who it was.

Sleep had eluded her. It was as though she had forgotten how. Ever since the party, she'd felt her heart racing. She'd tried taking deep breaths but couldn't seem to get enough oxygen. She desperately wished for sleep as a way of escaping herself and the miserable situation, at least for a while.

Uncle Nick had called Tig's mom and told her everything, but Tig had refused her parents' many offers of counsel, responding with a pointed "I don't want to talk about it." That evening, though, Tig heard a gentle shave-and-a-haircut knock at her door. She sat up in bed. "Come in, BD." Her mom had called in the big guns.

"How's my sweetie?" BD said, sitting down next to her on the bed.

"I don't want to talk about it."

"Is it a boy? You tell BD. I'll whoop him." Tig was sure BD already knew what had happened, but he wanted her to tell him.

Tig settled into her grandfather's arms. He had a way of making her feel safe, and before she knew it, she was spilling her guts about her humiliation, and sobbing into the sleeve of BD's soft flannel shirt.

"Oh, is that all?" he asked.

"Is that all?" Tig asked incredulously. "Isn't that enough?"

"Shoot. Reminds me of the time I tried to sing lead for the Orbits."

Tig looked confused. "I thought you always said you couldn't sing lead," she said.

"I can't," he replied. "But how do you think I found that out? Trial and error. And, boy, was it an error!

"I guess it was about 1963. The Orbits got a gig at a dive called the Jungle Club down around Five Points — where that drugstore is now. I decided I wanted to sing 'Party Doll.' Jerry and the rest of the guys said that was fine. We rehearsed it, and the night of the gig, I started singing. It didn't go well."

"Did people boo you and tell you your band stunk?"

"No, it was worse than that. At least that would have been over quickly. No, they just started getting up, one by one, and leaving. At first I thought maybe a couple of people were just going to the bathroom. So I kept on singing. By the time I was done, not a living soul was in that club anymore!

"So I said to Jerry, 'What happened?' and he said, 'You can't sing lead.' So I said, 'Well, why didn't you tell me that before I made a fool of myself?' And Jerry said, 'Because we were afraid you'd get mad and quit the band, and you're the only one with a van big enough to fit our equipment into'!" BD laughed.

"No way!" Tig said. "What did you do?"

"I'll tell you what I didn't do. I didn't sing 'Party Doll' . . . or lead on anything else . . . ever again!"

Tig smiled. She appreciated that BD sort of understood. But this was different. "At least you humiliated yourself in 1963 to a roomful of people. This is the Internet age, BD. My shame is worldwide, on the Web, forever."

"You're right," BD said. "It is different. I know it's a lot harder growing up now than it was when I was a boy. I wish I knew how to break the Internet for you."

Tig laughed. BD couldn't even figure out how to transfer his contacts to a new phone. But she knew that if he could, he really would break the Internet, just for her.

Tig thought of how much everyone loved BD. If he could make a fool of himself with his band and laugh about it years later, well, maybe she could too. Even if it was on the Internet. After all, there were worse things on the Web than one crummy band performance. There was so much new material every day that probably in a few weeks the video of her humiliation would be hiding in plain sight—still there, but abandoned and forgotten old news. One day maybe Tig would laugh about it like BD laughed about his "Party Doll" story. One day. But not yet.

After BD left, Tig wasn't quite through wallowing in her misery, so she stayed in her room for the remainder of the night.

The next day, Tig was allowed to skip Sunday lunch at her grandparents' house. The official reason was to continue to work on her science project, but the underlying one was that Tig still needed some time to collect herself.

With her parents and her younger sibs out of the house, Tig soaked in the absolute quiet. Here, walls surrounded her, protecting her from the looks, taunts, and snickers she would face at school on Monday. She was tempted to look at her phone or social media to know for certain what people were saying about her and the band, but she couldn't face it. It might be worse than she imagined. Maybe they hadn't sounded as bad as it seemed. Tig wished she could believe that, but she knew better.

On her bedside table lay one of her pairs of drumsticks.

She looked at them, then pressed them into her hands, running her fingers along their smooth surfaces. Part of her wanted to break them over her knee and throw them in the garbage. The drums had been the cause of all her misery at school. She thought back to how she'd wanted people to pay attention to her, to think she was special in some way . . . to think she was cool. She had hated being invisible. Now she wished she could return to invisibility.

She took the sticks and threw them against the wall. The pronounced bang and the clanging of wood against wood as they fell together to the floor startled her even though she'd expected the loud noise. She stared at the sticks as they rolled, one off the rug and under her bed and the other next to her backpack. *I'll leave them there and never pick them up again,* she told herself. *I'm through with the drums.*

But only a few moments passed before Tig was reaching under her bed, patting her hand on the rug and around various shoes, in search of the missing stick. When she had both of them in her grasp again, she studied them for damage.

Before she could fully think about what she was doing and why, Tig found herself in the studio. She sat on her little stool, put her feet on the pedals, and began pounding out rhythms. She played loudly, forcefully. Not a song per se, but different combinations of backbeats. Behind her drums, she could feel herself start to breathe again, like a fish tossed back into its bowl after a few seconds out of water.

Tig realized that no matter the amount of misery the drums might cause her, she couldn't give them up. She wasn't good yet, but she would keep playing. Years from now, when she could barely remember the names

Regan or Haley or Sofia, she would still be somewhere sitting behind some drums, a backbeat pounding in her brain and coming out her limbs.

The drums were no longer a means to an end or a silly little project.

They had become part of her.

Chapter Thirty-Four

"**W**here have you been?" Kyra demanded when Tig got to school Monday. She was sitting in the gym with Robbie and Olivia. "I had to have Mama call Aunt Julie last night just so I could make sure you were still alive! Do you have any idea how many texts I sent you?"

"Eleven," Tig said. "I also received six from Olivia, three from Will, and one big *Seriously?* from Robbie."

"Seemed like a valid question," Robbie said. "Man, you skip town just once for your great-grandma's party, and the world goes crazy."

"It is a good question," Kyra said. "So, seriously?

You storm off the stage like a crazy person and then you drop off the face of the planet. What are we supposed to think?"

"Correction. I did not storm off the stage like a crazy person. I stormed off the stage like a very mentally stable person who realized she'd made a complete fool of herself."

"Whatever you want to call it, Mama was furious."

Like I care, Tig wanted to say. But before she could come up with any response at all, Regan was upon her.

"Good morning, rock 'n' roll princess!" she said. Naturally, Haley and Sofia were on her heels. It was as though they were three parts of one organism.

Tig wanted to say something smart back to Regan, but she didn't. She was humiliated, and her role now was to stand there and take what Regan dished out. She'd earned it.

"Not so mouthy today, are we?" Regan said. "I can't blame you. There's really nothing left for you to say. Wow. *What* a train wreck! You must be so embarrassed. I mean, telling everyone you have a band and then it's all over YouTube that you can't even play one stupid song."

Okay, so maybe Tig wasn't so great at the whole standing-there-and-taking-it bit.

"If you knew anything about music," Tig replied, "you would know that 'Gotcha' isn't a stupid song; it's a difficult song, an advanced song. And that it's hard to play any song when your lead singer gets sick and your usual guitarist is out of town."

"Excuses, excuses," Regan said. "I'm just so glad that your big mouth got you into exposing your talentless, pathetic excuse for a band to the whole school."

"The whole world, really," Haley added. "My, my, but I do love the Internet!"

"If you love the Internet so much," Tig said, "then why don't you put up a video of yourself singing? I'd love to read all the comments about your supposed talent."

"I have too much class to self-promote," Haley said.

"Trust me, two things you'll never have to worry

about having too much of are class and talent," Tig replied.

"Haley's not putting any videos on YouTube," Regan said. "Because if she did, people would be talking about her video instead of yours." Tig was disappointed that Regan could see through her so easily. Regan continued, "And we want to make sure your video gets talked about around here for a very long time."

"Tig! There you are!" Will made his way to her from across the gym.

"Oh, look, it's your boyfriend the guitarist!" Regan said.

"Will is not my boyfriend," Tig said.

Olivia shifted her weight onto her opposite hip.

"He's not much of a guitarist either," said Regan. "We'll just leave you lovebirds alone . . . for now."

The Bots went to their usual section, and Will sat down next to Tig. "You okay?" he asked. "I've been worried about you."

"Life couldn't be better," Tig said. "Haven't you

heard? I'm a rock star."

"You and me both," Will said. "That was pretty embarrassing."

"Will, you were so great up there Friday night!" Olivia said.

"No, I wasn't," Will said. "I shouldn't have said I could play guitar. If Robbie'd been there instead of me, this never would've happened."

"But I couldn't be there, and you stepped up," Robbie said. "That means something."

"She's right," Olivia said. "You're very sweet."

The funny thing was, Tig thought so, too. Will was sweet. He'd made a complete fool of himself right along with her, even though he didn't have to, and instead of blaming her for screwing up the song and walking off the stage or even being mad at her for ignoring his texts, here he was, being all nice. She tried to remember what she'd always found so annoying about him, but she couldn't.

"I guess you've seen YouTube?" Robbie asked Tig.

"No," Tig replied. "I'm making a conscious decision

not to look."

"Good idea," Robbie said. "It's not pretty."

"You know what they say about denial," Tig said.

"It ain't just a river in Egypt," said Will.

"Exactly. But pretending it didn't happen doesn't solve the problem."

"You mean of being the laughingstock of the whole school and the rest of the city?" Kyra asked.

"No," Tig said. "I can deal with that. I mean, don't get me wrong—that part stinks, no question. But I think we have an even bigger problem."

"What?" asked Kyra.

"Has anybody heard from Claire?"

Chapter Thirty-Five

Claire hadn't shown up for school that day.

"She's probably still sick," Robbie said.

"Let's call her and find out," Kyra said.

"I'm too scared," Tig replied. "I mean, what if we call and she doesn't want to talk to us? What if she saw the video and has decided to ditch us?"

"Come on," Olivia said. "Claire's our friend."

"Is she?" Tig asked. "Or were we just her only option?" Tig hoped Olivia was right. She really liked Claire; she wanted them to be real friends.

"Let's just call her after school and check on her,"

Olivia said.

"Yeah, we can't *not* call her," Robbie said. "That would make us pretty inconsiderate friends, and then I wouldn't blame her for ditching us."

"Y'all are right," Tig replied. "We'll talk more about it at lunch."

As the girls went to their classes, a deep voice called behind Tig: "Miss Ripley?"

Tig turned around to see Mr. Ellis standing in the door of the science lab. Oh no. She'd completely forgotten about doing the science project over the weekend. She walked toward him, a sick feeling in her stomach.

"Good morning, Mr. Ellis," she said sheepishly.

"Good morning," he replied. "I just wondered if you needed to drop off your science project so you wouldn't have to try to shove it into your locker or carry it around all day."

"Yes, sir. About that . . . ," Tig began. "I had every intention of getting that done this weekend, but I had something kind of . . . traumatic . . . happen, and—"

"And let me guess. No project?"

"No, sir."

"Tig, this just isn't like you," Mr. Ellis said. "You've always been such a conscientious student."

"I'm really sorry, Mr. Ellis. I'll work harder. I promise."

The first bell rang. Students were pushing past her to get into the science lab. She needed to get to her first class before the tardy bell. Tig felt that she should say something else, but she didn't know what. Mr. Ellis didn't say anything either. He was a tall, imposing man, but he never raised his voice in anger. Tig almost wished he would. The disappointment on his face made her feel worse than if he'd lit into her.

I can't think about any of that right now, Tig told herself as she hurried to class. *I'll worry about the science project tonight when I can do something about it.* Meanwhile, she still had to get through the day and figure out what was going on with Claire.

At lunch the girls and Will brainstormed what Tig should say when she called Claire. "You could just say,

Hey, you still alive, or what?" Kyra said. "Keep it light."

"Or: *I've been so concerned about you. Is everything okay?*" Olivia said. "And then see if she brings up the band. Or the YouTube video."

"Maybe instead of calling, we should just go by and see how she's doing?" Robbie said. "Take her some ice pops or something. Mono gives you a sore throat, right?"

"You know what's good?" Will said. "Those lime juice ice pops."

"Those are good!" Olivia said.

"So let's do it," said Robbie. "We'll meet at Tig's house. I'm sure Mrs. Ripley will be glad to chauffeur us."

"I guess she would," Tig said.

"Text me later and let me know how it goes," Will said to Tig. She felt her face flush and wondered if Olivia noticed.

After school the four girls met at Tig's house and, as expected, Tig's mother was happy to drive them, both to Publix to pick up ice pops and to Claire's to deliver them.

"Shouldn't we have called first?" Kyra whispered to Tig in the van. "Isn't it rude to just show up?"

"It's a surprise," Tig said. But the truth was, Tig was afraid that a one-on-one phone call would simply result in awkward silence, and that would make her feel stupid, and she'd had quite enough of feeling stupid over the past few days. At least this way, there were three other girls to fill in any conversation gaps.

Tig's mother sat in the car while the four girls went up to the door. "We won't be long," Tig told her.

They rang the doorbell. Claire's mother answered. "Oh, how lovely!" she said in a Mary Poppins voice. "Do come in and say hello! Poppet, you have more visitors!"

Tig wondered for a second why Claire's mother had used the word *more*, but before she could process it, Mrs. Roberts was leading them into the family room, where Claire was sitting in her pajamas on the couch . . .

With Regan, Haley, and Sofia gathered around her.

Chapter Thirty-Six

"**W**hat are you doing here?" Tig said. She knew it was rude. She hadn't even said hello to Claire. But she couldn't help herself.

"We're visiting our friend Claire," Regan said. "What are *you* doing here?"

"Visiting *our* friend Claire." Tig knew it sounded petty, like in second grade when kids thought they owned their friends and no one else could be friends with them.

"Hey, Tig," Claire said. "Hey, Kyra, Robbie, Olivia. I'd hug you, but I might still be a little contagious.

Doctor says it's okay as long as you don't get too close."

"We brought you some ice pops," Robbie said, awkwardly shoving the box in front of Claire.

"Oh, thanks," Claire said. "Mum, could you put these in the freezer?"

Suddenly the lime ice pops looked pretty meager. "We brought Claire this get-well basket," Regan said. The basket was huge and pink and wrapped up in cellophane with a glittery bow. Inside were all manner of froufrou snacks and groovy, retro-looking fruit sodas.

"So how was your party, Kyra?" Claire asked. "I'm so sorry I missed it."

"Funny you should ask," Regan said. "I was just about to show you a video on YouTube. . . ."

"We have to go," Tig said.

"But you just got here," said Claire. "Can't you stay a little longer?"

"Wish we could," Tig said. "But my mom's in the car, so you know how it is."

"Well, all right then," said Claire. "It was good to

see you. Thanks for coming by."

"Yeah, you too," said Tig. "I mean, the seeing you part. Not the coming by part because you didn't come by; we did. I mean, not that you would come by because you're the one who's sick and everything, and—"

"So we'll see you soon," Robbie said, saving Tig from any further babbling.

Tig's mom was on the phone when the girls got back in the van, so they had an excuse to whisper. "They're trying to flip her," Tig said. "They didn't even know she was alive, but now that we want her to be our friend and be in the band, they want to take her away from us!"

"Maybe they're just being nice?" Olivia offered. "Oh, who am I kidding? You're right, Tig. They've flipped her. Claire was scared to sing lead before, and now, when they show her the video, she'll never do it again. It's over. She's with the Bots."

"This stinks," Robbie said. "The Bots are such jerks! We need Claire's voice!"

"Plus, I really like her," Olivia said.

CHAPTER THIRTY-SIX

"Me too," said Kyra.

"We all do," Tig said, and Robbie nodded. "Ugh! I hate this! Could somebody just shoot me, please, before my life gets any worse?"

"Thank you so much," Tig's mom said. She hung up. "Tig, we're going to drop your friends off now."

"But I thought we were all going to get supper?" Tig said.

"Not anymore," her mother replied.

"But, Mom," Tig said, "we'd all planned—"

"I'm taking the girls home, Tig," her mom said. "The person I was just talking to on the phone? That was Mr. Ellis."

Chapter Thirty-SEven

They dropped Olivia off last. She hugged Tig and wished her luck.

When Tig and her mother were alone in the car, Tig braced herself for the lecture of a lifetime.

But it didn't come. Instead they drove home in silence. That was worse. Tig's mother was rarely one to be rendered speechless. If she wasn't talking, she must be really upset. Like *beyond* upset.

When they got home, Tig's mother kissed the little ones and told them to go play. "Dave, we have a situation," she told Tig's dad.

They sat Tig down in the formal living room, which no one ever used, and Tig's mother relayed the information to her dad. "She just didn't turn it in. Nothing! Zilch! I can't . . . I mean . . . What?" She put her head in her hands. "What were you thinking?"

"I meant to do it," Tig said. "But Kyra told everyone at school that our band was playing at her party, and we weren't ready anyway, and then Robbie and Claire couldn't make it, so—"

"So you cancel. Boom. Easy!" said her mom.

"I tried to. But then Regan smack-talked me in the lunch room, and I kinda said, *Oh yes, we would play*, and then I had to."

"Then that's it. Good-bye, band. Hello, studying," her mother replied.

"Mom! I can't quit the band! I'm the leader!"

"Antigone Ripley, you have an F right now in science class. An F! There is no discussion. You are grounded from the band until your next progress report. And you will not use your phone or your computer for any social purposes until then either.

Do you understand?" Her mother's jaw was tight, her lips pursed.

"Dad?" Tig said. He was generally the good cop to her mom's bad cop. But not this time.

"Don't look at me," her dad said. "Your mom's right. An F's an F."

That was when it all hit her.

Not only was Tig a joke at school . . . not only was she a laughingstock on the Internet . . . not only was her band a failure . . . not only had her new friend Claire ditched her . . . but now she was failing science, too. And to be honest, the rest of her grades weren't so hot either. She had ruined everything she had going for her only to fail miserably as a musician. Tig started to cry.

"If this is a ploy, it's not going to work," said her mom. "You're not getting out of this just by turning on the waterworks."

But as Tig kept crying, her mom softened. "Honey, this just isn't like you," said her mom. "You were always so responsible and so on top of your schoolwork. I know you like your little band, but you've got to find a balance."

"It's not just the band," Tig said. She told them everything: all about Regan turning everyone against her, how she had to stand up to Regan to prove herself, how it had all gone horribly wrong and wound up on the Internet, and how Claire had decided to become a Bot instead of her friend.

Even though she was too big for his lap anymore, Tig's dad held her until she ran out of tears. Her mother patted her back and stroked her hair, whispering, "Now, now, sweetie . . . it's going to be okay." Then she asked, "Dave, isn't there some way we can contact the person in charge of the Internet and have that awful video removed?"

It was so ridiculous, Tig couldn't help but laugh. Her dad did, too.

"What? Why is that funny?" asked her mom.

"Mom, there's no one 'in charge of' the Internet," Tig said.

"But you know," said her dad, "we could flag the

video and ask YouTube to remove it. They might not, but all they can say is no, and then we're no worse off than we were before."

Tig doubted it would do much good—she felt sure that YouTube would consider the request trivial— but it made her feel better to know that her parents would try to do what they could to help. Even though they were upset with her, they were still on her side. At least somebody was.

There was just one more thing Tig wanted to know. "Mom, can I still play the drums?"

Tig's mom looked at her dad. He shrugged.

"Well . . . ," she said. "I mean, I have paid for your lessons through the end of the semester, and it wouldn't be fair to Lee to ask for a refund. So I suppose you can go to your lessons if your dad thinks it's okay."

"Okay by me," said her dad.

"Can I practice?"

Tig's mom looked at her dad. He said, "I suppose so. But only after you've finished all your homework and studied for tests. Not a second before. Not even for study breaks."

"Fair enough," Tig replied.

"What's say we get started on your science project?" her dad said.

That sounded like the best idea Tig had heard all day.

Chapter Thirty-Eight

Once the science project was turned in, Tig had the unfortunate task of telling the other girls that her parents had nixed band practice for the next few weeks. She wondered if they'd be upset . . . or relieved.

"So, long story short, no phone, no texting, no social media . . . and, worst of all, no band practice," Tig explained. "I can still practice by myself after all my homework is finished, and I still get to go to my lessons, but there's no group practice until progress reports come out and my grades are back up."

"My parents would have done the exact same

thing," Olivia said. "Either that or just killed me. I can't believe you didn't turn in your science project!"

"Take it easy," Tig said. "I've already had enough lecturing from my folks."

Olivia smiled. "Sorry. But, wow. That's big. You'll get your grades up soon, right?"

"I'm fine with taking some time off from practicing," Kyra said. Robbie rolled her eyes at Tig. It wasn't like Kyra ever practiced anyway.

"Okay, let's say Tig brings her grades up," Robbie said. "Then what?"

"What do you mean?" Tig asked.

"I mean, what difference does it make right now, anyway? We still don't know if we have a lead singer. So is there even a band?"

"Well, sure there is," Tig said.

Just then Kyra spilled her cling peaches onto the table, so she got up to get some napkins. Olivia began talking to Will. Robbie leaned in and whispered to Tig. "I don't know, Ripley. Have you ever wondered if maybe this band is more trouble than it's worth?"

"The thought did occur to me this past weekend when the entire world came crashing down," Tig replied.

"We can't have a band unless we have a real commitment from all the members," Robbie continued. "Claire, at best, is on the fence, but probably out altogether; Kyra's halfhearted about the whole thing; Olivia's good, but eventually her tennis schedule is going to become a problem, and you? You're so all in, you can't handle your regular life anymore. This can't all rest on you. There's got to be buy-in from everybody."

"Just give it some time," Tig said. "Please, Robbie? If you bail, then there really won't be a band anymore. Please hang in there with me."

Robbie sighed. "Okay, but you better get those grades up. And next time you have problems like the science project, let me know so I can help."

Tig agreed. "Thanks for sticking with me," she told Robbie.

"No problem," Robbie replied. "I just hope Claire does the same."

Chapter Thirty-Nine

Being in the lunch room seemed less painful now that it was Tig's only social outlet. She hadn't sent a text in two whole days, and she was sure her thumbs were going through withdrawal. Every so often one of them would spasm as she held her pencil in math class, as though it wanted to say, *Remember what fun we used to have together?*

The good news was that Mr. Ellis had given her a 70 percent on her science project. It was a good one. (Having a dad who was a mechanical engineer came in handy in times like this.) If she'd turned the project in on time, it would've gotten her a 100, but she was lucky Mr. Ellis accepted it at all, and she knew it. With her daily grades and a test coming up the following week, Tig knew she could be back in B territory before progress reports. Then she'd be free from this purgatory.

The other good news was that most everyone at school had grown tired of the jabs about the band and had gone back to tormenting other kids about their acne or weight. Well, it was good news for Tig. Not so much for the usual targets.

And still other good news was that Claire had fully recovered and was back at school.

Except this wasn't entirely good news.

On her first day back, Claire had made apologies to the Pandora's Box crowd and then had sat with the Bots at lunch. She'd promised she'd be back the next day, but from the looks of how tight she and the Bots seemed, Tig and the others had their doubts.

"She fits right in," Olivia said. "She's well dressed, pretty—"

"Too pretty," Robbie said. "Regan won't be able to stand for that very long. She doesn't like to be upstaged."

"But by then Claire will have forgotten all about us," Olivia said. "She'll have already been sucked into their machine, and she won't come back to us. She'll just stay in their clique and act out the frenemies dramas over and over like they all do."

"Instead of singing with our band," Robbie said. "What a waste."

"Let's not get too carried away," Kyra said. "Claire might not do any of that."

Tig rolled her eyes. Of all the hypocrisy. Kyra would be the first to fall prey to the Bots' machinations, if only they noticed she was alive long enough to let her into their group.

But the next day Claire did sit with the band at lunch. Tig could hardly believe it.

Everyone tried to act normal, but Tig felt she could've reached out and touched the awkward vibe that hung in the air. The Pandora's Box girls were careful about everything they said, almost as though Claire were some sort of rare, delicate curiosity that they had to tiptoe around in a museum. Even Robbie was devoid of her usual who-gives-a-rip attitude and had morphed into a sort of frozen-smile, 1950s housewife creature.

"So, you're feeling better?" Robbie asked Claire, a weird smile plastered across her face.

"Yes, thanks," Claire said. "Mono was no picnic."

Robbie started laughing. "Hahahahahaha! Picnic! Good one!" Tig shot her a take-it-down-a-notch look. Robbie cleared her throat and took a huge bite of her sandwich.

"What did you do all that time you were out of school?" Kyra asked.

"Nothing, really. I was so exhausted, all I could do was lie around."

Before anyone could ask a follow-up question, Regan came up behind Claire and hugged her around the neck. "Clairesy!" she said.

"Hi, Regan," Claire replied.

CHAPTER THIRTY-NINE

"You're sitting with us again tomorrow, right?"

"Okay, sure," Claire said.

"And this weekend you're going shopping with us?"

"Yes, Birmingham." Tig liked the way Claire said *BUR-ming-um*, glossing over the *ham*.

"Oh, and what was that thing your mother used for your sore muscles?"

"Regan, please," Claire said, blushing.

"Come on! Say it!"

"All right," Claire said. "A hot water bottle." It was the most British-sounding thing Tig had ever heard: it sounded like *hawt wawtah bawtuhl*.

Regan clapped her hands and squealed. "See you in a bit!"

The girls looked at Claire. "Apparently, I've created a bit of a catchphrase," she said.

"Getting along well with Regan and Haley, huh?" Tig said. She just couldn't stand it any longer.

"They've been very kind." Claire said the word as *bean* instead of *ben*.

Tig wanted to ask Claire if the Bots had told her

not to be friends with her and the other girls in the band, but she was afraid of sounding needy and petty, so she let it go.

By the day's end Tig had heard at least a dozen people stop Claire in the hall to get her to say *hot water bottle*.

"Who knew the masses were so easily amused?" Tig asked Robbie when they heard some kids in the hall mimicking Claire's new "catchphrase."

"They're making her feel special," Robbie said. "All part of sucking her in. And, of course, away from Pandora's Box."

Tig wanted to shrug off Robbie's assessment, tell her she was reading too much into things, but she couldn't.

Every time she heard someone else say *hot water bottle*, she could feel her new friend slipping away.

Chapter Forty

All weekend Tig worried about losing Claire. She had sat with them at lunch exactly twice the previous week, and both times had felt awkward and strained.

Robbie had eventually mustered the courage to ask her what she'd heard about the disaster at Kyra's party, but Claire had brushed it off as though it were no big deal.

"One hears things," Claire had said. "But no matter." Kyra had even gone so far as to ask Claire if she'd watched the YouTube video, but Claire said she hadn't. Tig wondered why not; she didn't think she would've been able to resist watching someone else from school crash and burn like that. She wondered if Claire had really watched the video but was trying to be kind. Claire was very kind, after all. . . . Clearly, she was too kind to tell the Pandora's Box girls to buzz off now that she was friends with a higher social class.

The worst part of turning all this over and over in her head was that Tig couldn't agonize over and dissect it with her friends because she was grounded. Tig's mother had assured her that everyone in her generation had survived growing up without texting, cell phones, and social media, but Tig couldn't fathom what they had done with themselves. She'd already done all her homework and practiced drums for a full hour. "Read a book," her mother had said. When Tig whined, her mother suggested various household chores, so Tig pretended to take a sudden interest in a novel and then retired to her bedroom. But instead of reading, she lay across the bed and obsessed about her friends and the band.

When she came down to the kitchen, Tig was

assigned to set the table. Her mother handed her six plates from the cupboard. "Why six?" Tig asked.

"Uncle Paul's joining us," said her mother. "Kate and the kids are in Montgomery, visiting her family."

At dinner that night Uncle Paul told stories about his university students. "So I told her, no, you can't turn your assignment in late! And if you ever come to my office again with such an outrageous request, I will ban you from office hours altogether!"

Tig's dad shook his head and laughed. "I'm glad I wasn't in your class."

"You'd never have made it," Uncle Paul said, punching Tig's dad lightly on the shoulder. "But speaking of my class, I have a little proposition for you. Or more specifically, for Tig."

"Me?" Tig asked. "What do you mean?"

"You know we have Ad Comp coming up soon," Uncle Paul said. Of course they were all familiar with that. Uncle Paul had for years been the faculty advisor for Ad Comp. It was a big national competition where college teams competed to see who could come up with the best advertising campaign for a bogus product. One year it had been a car that ran on water; another year it was for doggie dental floss. Most of the time, UA's team won, largely because Uncle Paul was a creative genius and also because he rode his team like a drill sergeant.

"Yes," Tig said. "I know about the competition. But what's that got to do with me?"

"This year's product is submarine pants."

"What are submarine pants?"

"Ridiculously high-waisted pants with suspenders. The team's challenge is to sell them to teenage girls as high-fashion items." He pulled out his phone and showed Tig a photograph of a World War I–era sailor wearing the goofy-looking pants.

"Um, nobody I know would wear those in a million years!" Tig said.

"Hence the challenge," Uncle Paul replied.

"Okay," Tig said. "But I still don't see what that's got to do with me."

"Well, my students decided that they wanted to

hire some teen models to lip-sync a song for the ad," said Uncle Paul. "The team's concept is to make a highly stylized video with girls pretending to play and sing this old seventies punk song called 'Submission.' But we can't spend money on models; the rules of the contest prohibit it. Remember that day I recorded your band playing 'Sweet Home Alabama'? I showed my class the video, and long story short, my students think you rock. They want y'all to be in their commercial."

"Oh, so you want Tig's band to lip-sync the song?" Tig's dad asked.

"No. That's the beauty of it," Uncle Paul said. "They can really play! Make room in the trophy case, 'cause UA's taking home another cup!"

"You mean we'd get to make our own video, and we wouldn't even have to pay for it?" Tig asked.

"Yep."

"Mom! Can we?" Tig was so excited, she could hardly think straight. Uncle Paul's students never did anything halfway. If they made a video, it would look superprofessional.

"When would they have to do it?" Tig's mother asked.

"End of next month," Uncle Paul said.

Tig's mother did some calculations on her fingers. "That won't give her enough time. She's grounded from the band until progress reports, and those don't come out until the twentieth."

"Mom, come on!" Tig said. "Can't you make an exception?"

"No, I can't," her mother replied. "And don't you and your uncle even bother trying to gang up on me and make me feel guilty. I told you your punishment, and I'm sticking to it."

"That would give her only about a week and a half to practice the song with the band," Tig's dad said.

"Don't you start in on me, too," Tig's mother said.

"Think you can get it together in a week and a half?" Uncle Paul asked.

"I don't know," Tig said.

"It will be great," Uncle Paul said. "Just think, once the competition is over, the college ad federation will post the video on YouTube, and all your friends at school will get to see it."

Suddenly Tig felt a sinking feeling in her stomach. YouTube. A video of her band. That hadn't worked out so well the last time.

A week and a half of practice? What if it wasn't enough time? What if someone had to be out of town again and couldn't do it? What if they made complete fools of themselves . . . again?

They wouldn't. Robbie would be with them this time, and she could rock anything. Especially seventies punk—she'd be all over that. And Claire! How great would her voice sound on a punk song?

That is, if Claire were still their lead singer. And lately that was looking like a very big if.

Tig was torn. If this went well, it would be a huge boon to the band and could undo the damage done at Kyra's party. If it didn't go well, it would be another nail in the coffin for Pandora's Box.

"Can I talk to the other girls and get back to you?" she asked her uncle.

"Of course," he replied.

If only Tig could use the phone or text! But it would have to wait until school. Tig wasn't sure if she hoped her friends would say yes or if she hoped they'd stop her from making another big mistake.

In the meantime Tig listened to "Submission" over and over. It was a great song, and she desperately wanted to play it. Punk was a new genre for her, and she loved the fierceness of it.

Ever since she'd taken up drums, Tig's thirst for music had become unquenchable. She'd researched the greatest drummers of all time on the Internet and had listened to their music and watched drum covers of her favorite songs from their bands. As a result, she was completely over the pop songs she used to listen to and had instead developed an eclectic taste in music that spanned several decades. She'd watched Buddy Rich and Viola Smith at BD's recommendation, and had even changed her ringtone to James Brown's "Funky Drummer." She repeatedly listened to her dad's copy of Led Zeppelin's IV on vinyl, admiring how their drummer was the engine that drove the band. She watched covers of the Rolling Stones' "Paint It Black" and wondered how anyone could move all four limbs that fast without taking off in flight. There was so much to learn, so much to take in! Tig wished school were half as interesting.

The only one who matched Tig's passion for music was Robbie. The two of them could talk for hours about bands and musicians. Olivia understood music from her training, and she enjoyed it, but her tastes were more in the pop realm, and Kyra just liked what everyone else liked. Robbie, Tig knew, would relish the opportunity to play seventies punk, but would Olivia and Kyra have any interest at all in this new venture? Tig hoped so. She could hardly wait to get to school the next day to get their reactions.

Chapter Forty-One

On Monday, when Robbie, Olivia, and Kyra were all settled in the gym before the first bell, Tig made the announcement. "I have some potentially exciting news," she said.

She told them all about Uncle Paul's proposition, explaining what Ad Comp was, the fake product they were charged with selling, and how they'd come up with the girl band concept and how Uncle Paul had suggested Pandora's Box play the song for the commercial. "They'll use the university's sound and video production stuff," she said. "No cost at all. It will look and sound really professional."

"If we sound really professional," Kyra said.

"Hey, what happened to Miss Positive Thinking?" Tig asked. "Can't somebody else come up with a hare-brained scheme now and then?"

Kyra smiled. "I'll give you that one."

"So, what do y'all think?" Tig said. "Do we take the opportunity or not?"

"I'm in," Kyra said. "Whatever you want. Besides, it won't be like we're playing live. We can do another take if we need to. They can edit it."

"Well, some," Tig said. "I think there's a limit to how much they can do. I mean, we can't stink. We've got to do it right."

"We won't stink," Robbie said. "I know that album. Cutting-edge. I can have it ready to go in a week. When can we practice together?"

"That's actually still an issue," Tig said. "My mom won't relent on my punishment. We'll have to practice separately until progress reports come out. Then we'll have a week and a half to get together and practice as a band."

"Yikes," Olivia said. "That's not a lot of time."

"I know," Tig said. "But if we all promise to work really hard individually, maybe we can make it work."

"What does Claire think about all this?" Robbie asked.

Tig grimaced. "I'll let you know when I find out."

Chapter Forty-Two

Tig couldn't wait.

All those times she'd waited for just the right moment to talk to Claire . . . about joining the band . . . about whether Regan had turned her against them . . . those were over. A new day had dawned for Tig, one where caution was overruled by a burning desire to play a kick-butt song with her kick-butt band. Well, they'd be kick-butt eventually, wouldn't they?

Tig couldn't wait. She had to know.

She caught Claire at her locker. No Regan, no Haley, no Sofia. Perfect timing.

"Ever hear of a band called the Sex Pistols?" Tig said, skipping any small talk or conversational niceties.

"Are you kidding?" Claire said. "My dad has a framed poster of their album cover in his office."

Yes! Tig thought. "Well, just imagine how proud your dear old dad would be if his daughter's band recorded one of their songs."

"The band? That's still on?"

Tig didn't like the way Claire's voice sounded—like she'd hadn't thought about the band in some time.

"Yeah, it's still on," Tig said. "I mean, I've been grounded for a while, but when progress reports come out, I'm good to go. We're going to record a song at the university—and make a video and everything. See, my uncle—"

"You wore it!" Tig turned around to see Regan. "I told you it was *so* your color!" Regan stroked the collar on Claire's sweater.

"Thanks!" Claire said. "I wasn't sure which

earrings to wear with it."

Regan linked her arm in Claire's. Tig could hear her saying, "Definitely the silver. Good choice," as the two of them walked away.

Chapter Forty-Three

"**S**o she just walks right off with them, talking about accessories," Tig said. "Regan gave full approval to the silver earrings, in case you were wondering."

"Oh, thank heavens!" Robbie said sarcastically. "Because what's more important than which earrings to wear?"

School had just gotten out, and Tig had to tell the whole story about Claire fast, before the bus or carpool took her bandmates away.

"I can't believe she asked if the band was still on," Olivia said. "Like we wouldn't have told her if we'd called the whole thing off?"

"What color was her sweater?" Kyra asked.

Everyone stared at her.

"What? You said Regan said it was her color. I just wondered."

"I guess this means we count Claire out, then," Robbie said. "Man, I sure hate it. What a waste of a perfectly killer voice."

"I hate to lose Claire, not just her voice," Olivia said. "I really like her."

"We all do," Tig said. "But she's one of them now, and there's nothing we can do about it."

"Maybe Claire can be friends with all of us," Kyra said. "Maybe all of us can be friends."

"Yeah, and maybe pink unicorns will sprinkle magical flowers all over the land!" Robbie said.

Tig smirked. "Give it up, Kyra. They don't want to be friends with us, and we don't want to be friends with them." Well, the rest of them didn't. Tig still couldn't fathom why Kyra was so desperate for their approval.

"What are we going to do about the Ad Comp

commercial?" Olivia asked. "Who's going to be our singer?"

"I don't know yet," Tig said. "But we'll figure something out."

"We have to," Robbie said. "The gauntlet has been thrown down. The Bots want to know if our band is 'still on'? We've got to show them it's *so* on!"

"Exactly," Tig said. "Are we all together on this?"

Olivia and Kyra nodded.

"Good," Tig said. "Because now, more than ever, I'm determined to make this work. Pandora's Box for the win!"

Chapter Forty-Four

"**S**ubmission" had a syncopated rhythm for the backbeat. That meant that Tig had to kick the bass on *one and*, the *and* of three, and the *and* of four. She thought she'd never get used to doing three kicks in succession when it was time to start over the measure.

But she would get it.

Claire or no Claire, Pandora's Box was going to make that Ad Comp commercial.

Lee was confident about Tig's ability to play the song. "It's not all that complicated once you get the hang of the syncopation," he said. "It's slower than 'Gotcha.'"

"I thought we agreed we'd never speak of that song again," Tig said.

Lee grinned. "Aw, come on. If you're going to lead a band, you're going to have to buck up," he said. "Everybody who plays music has at least one story of complete humiliation. It gives you something to talk about with other musicians when you're up at three a.m. after a gig. It builds character."

Tig remembered BD's "Party Doll" story and almost smiled. Almost. "I've built all the character I want to for a long time," she said. "I can't mess this one up. You think I'll be able to get it?"

"Tig, you're a good drummer for a beginner," Lee said. "What's more, you're determined and dedicated. With practice, you can do anything. Just take it slowly until you master the coordination, then get the tempo."

For the next couple of lessons, Lee and Tig worked on her opening cymbal crashes (which were pretty easy, except that Tig's kit didn't have a crash cymbal, so she had to do everything on the ride cymbal), the backbeat, and the drum fill. Once she mastered the syncopation, the rest fell into place fairly easily. By the third lesson since they'd started the song, she could play most of the way through without messing up.

"Good—keep going," Lee said. As Tig banged away on the backbeat, Lee settled down with his guitar. Almost as soon as he started, Tig lost her count and got so flustered, she had to stop altogether.

It was just like the night of Kyra's party.

"Why do I do that?" Tig said. "I was doing just fine!"

"The guitar part is on a counter rhythm," Lee said. "Makes it a little tricky."

"I'll say," Tig said. "Let's try it again."

They ran through it a few more times before Tig's lesson was over, and later that night, after she'd finished all her homework, Tig practiced it with the song playing through headphones.

"I've almost got it," Tig told the crew at lunch. "Just in time for progress reports. How're you guys doing?"

"I'm cool," Olivia said.

"Ready to rock," said Robbie.

"I'm still practicing," Kyra said.

Will was, of course, sitting by Sam, right across from Tig. He looked at her as if to say, *Good luck with that*. Tig nodded.

"Progress reports come out tomorrow," Tig said. "I've got a solid B in science, so I'm golden. Practice at my house on Friday, then?"

"Aren't you forgetting one very important detail?" asked Robbie. "We're short a lead singer."

Claire hadn't sat at the lunch table all week. And the few times she'd talked to the girls in class or between, she'd never mentioned the band or the video. Tig had been too proud to bring it up again. She didn't want Regan to get wind of anything, and revel in her desperation.

"I still say you should do it, Robbie," Tig said. "I'm sure they can auto-tune you or something. Besides, it's mostly growling, isn't it?"

"I will not be auto-tuned like some cheap, no-talent pop star," Robbie said. "If it's so easy, you do it."

"I'm not good enough to sing and keep count,"

Tig said. "If you want proof of that, there's this very enlightening YouTube video you may have heard something about."

"What about you, Olivia?" Robbie asked. "Think you've got it in you to growl?"

"Olivia's not the growling type," Will said. "She's way too sweet."

Tig noticed that Olivia and Will looked at each other, then blushed and quickly looked away. What was up with that?

"He has a point," Tig said, somewhat distracted. She forced herself to get back to the matter at hand. "What if we did an instrumental?"

Just then Claire approached their table. "Is there room for one more?" she asked.

"Um, sure," Tig said. "It's just that . . . well, I didn't think you were sitting with us anymore."

"Don't be silly," Claire said. "Of course I want to sit with my friends."

"We're still your friends?" Robbie asked. "I thought you'd thrown us over for . . . a better offer."

Everyone stared at Robbie. "What? It's what we were all thinking."

"I never meant it that way, honestly," Claire said. "Regan can be somewhat—"

"Evil?" Olivia said.

"Malicious?" Robbie offered.

"I was going to say . . . exclusive, perhaps," Claire said. "She was very kind to befriend me, and she was quite solicitous about my well-being when I was ill, but she became easily annoyed if I didn't spend all my time with her group. I didn't want to hurt her feelings, and well, you all seemed to manage without me."

"We didn't manage," Tig said. "The fact is, Claire, we didn't want to freak you out or seem clingy, but we miss you. We miss your friendship. And to be completely honest, we miss you in the band."

"Then you'll still let me sing?" Claire asked.

"*Let* you?" Robbie said. "Uh, yeah. We'll allow you to do that. Like, please, please, pleeeeze?"

Claire grinned. "Good. Because I really want to. I've missed you all. And I've missed the band, even though I'm still a little scared of the idea of singing in front of people. It never seemed so bad when you guys were with me, though. It felt like fun."

"So you're still in?" Tig could feel her cheeks getting sore from smiling so big.

"Oh yes," Claire said. "And I especially want to sing in the video."

"You do?" Tig said.

"Absolutely!"

"I was afraid the whole video idea had scared you off," Tig said. "You know, with the stage fright thing. I thought maybe the idea of being recorded had you so spooked that you'd never come back."

"Well, the video does scare me a bit," Claire said. "But I don't have much of a choice, really."

"What do you mean?" asked Robbie.

"You see, Regan . . . She'd already tried to talk me out of singing with the band. But then it seemed she'd overheard Tig telling me about the video. And then . . . she forbade me to do it."

"She *what?*" said Robbie.

"Yes. So you see, I have to sing on the video. I can't let it sit, some twit telling me what I can and can't do." Tig loved the way Claire said *cahnt*. She loved even more the way Claire had just called Regan a twit.

"Did you just call Regan a twit?" Robbie said.

Obviously, Tig wasn't the only one who'd enjoyed that part.

"Yes, sorry," Claire said.

"Don't apologize on our account!" Robbie replied.

"It's just that it does make me angry when someone tells me I can't do something. I have this—oh, I don't know, perhaps it's a personality flaw—but I just feel that I must do the exact opposite in order to assert myself. Do you think I'm quite horrible?"

"We think you're wonderful," Tig said. "Don't we?" Everyone agreed. "Glad to have you back, Claire. Friday night, everybody: My house. Sleepover. Lots of practice!"

After the reunited band exchanged fist bumps, Tig looked over her shoulder. Regan and Haley were staring a hole straight through the girls of Pandora's Box.

Chapter Forty-Five

"I think I may have this thing framed," Tig said. Progress reports had just been handed out a few minutes before the last bell. Tig's had all As except for a B in science. Amazing what she could do when she was motivated.

"Your mom just might frame it," Kyra said. "My dad said she's been checking your grades every day on the school's Web portal, just to make sure you haven't slipped."

"Dad's going to be even happier than she is," Tig replied. "He said that Saturday morning he'd fix us all a big brunch whenever we got up."

"Belgian waffles?" Kyra asked.

"Depends," Tig said. "Am I going to be pleased with your progress? And I don't mean your grades."

"I'm doing my best," Kyra said. "I can't practice all the time."

Tig had already quizzed Lee on how difficult Kyra's part would be. He'd said that of all the parts, the bass was easiest, and that Kyra should be able to get it down if she practiced daily.

Before Tig could lecture Kyra about her lack of dedication to her instrument, the bell rang. The two cousins met Olivia, Robbie, and Claire out front at the carpool area. Claire had brought her overnight bag to school and was riding home with Tig, since she was the only one who didn't have to go home and get an instrument. "Come over as soon as you can," Tig told the other three girls. "Claire and I are ready to get started."

"Me too," Robbie said. "Man, I love this song! Such a great riff. I can't wait to crank it out!"

"I've got to get my hair done before we make the video," Kyra said. "Maybe some highlights right here. What do you think?"

"I think you'd do better to worry more about your bass line and less about your hair," Tig said.

"Kyra's got a point, though," Robbie said. "Video is a powerful medium for bands. It's not just about sound; it's about look and image, too." Robbie got a gleam in her eye as she studied Tig. "Have you ever thought about dyeing your hair?"

"To what?"

"I don't know—pink?"

"Pink hair?" Tig replied. "As if my mom and dad are going to let me get pink hair!"

"There are worse things," Robbie said. "Besides, now that you've got that shiny new progress report to show them, it might be the best time ever to ask."

"I am not dyeing my hair pink!"

"Of course you're not," Robbie said. "Not all of it, anyway."

"We can figure all this out later," Claire said. "Right

now all I can focus on is that our band is making a video!"

"You're still doing the video?"

It was Regan.

"Don't even start," Tig said.

"Claire, you've got to be kidding me," Regan said. "You're not actually going to be filmed with these losers, are you? It's social suicide!"

"I've already told you, Regan, my friends are not losers."

"Have it your way," Regan said. "But once you do this, Claire, I wash my hands of you. If you change your mind before you humiliate yourself, call me. There's still room for you in our group. But once you publicly associate yourself with this band, that door closes. Forever."

"Do you realize how absurd you sound?" Claire asked. "You can't actually expect to tell people what to do."

"That's exactly what I expect," Regan said. "Haley and Sofia and the other girls in our group appreciate my advice."

"Demands and advice aren't the same thing, Regan!" Claire said. "That's not what friendship is about. Friends are supposed to support one another."

"Friends are supposed to keep their friends from turning into dorks," Regan said. "Come on! Look at these people. Do they look like rock stars to you?" She looked each girl up and down, motioning with her hand. When she got to Robbie, with her hot-pink purse, distressed jeans, and a bandanna tied around her ankle, plus plaid high-top tennis shoes with black laces, a bright blue top, razor-layered shiny black hair with the purple streak, and cherry lips, she had little choice but to concede. "Okay, maybe this one." Robbie couldn't help but smirk. "But look at the other ones. Rock stars? Really? Claire, you're going to look like a fool next to these fools. You already know they can't play, and if you would just watch that YouTube nightmare like I told you to, you'd know they have no stage presence to pull off a music video! As your friend, I simply *have* to intervene."

"Rubbish!" Claire replied. "Your idea of friendship

is turning people into . . . into—"

"The word you're looking for is *Bots*," Tig said.

"Bots," Claire said. "I'm sorry, Regan. But I'm not interested in becoming one of your Bots."

"Suit yourself, then," Regan said. "Just don't come crying to me when this whole thing blows up in your face. You're sealing your own social destiny."

When Regan was gone, Tig said, "Don't let her get into your head, y'all."

But on the car ride home, as Claire made small talk with Tig's mom, Tig did some serious thinking.

Robbie and Kyra had actually made a very good point: the girls didn't look the part yet. And they'd been so busy practicing the song, no one had even thought about stage presence.

It was one thing for Robbie and Kyra to say it, but when Regan made the same point, Tig knew the situation would have to be remedied.

Chapter Forty-Six

Tig's palms were sweating a little bit when everyone was plugged in, tuned up, and ready to practice the song together for the first time. She had waited for this moment for weeks. Pounding out the backbeat alone day after day, she could hardly wait to hear what it would sound like when they all played together.

She counted off with her sticks, and Robbie cranked the guitar. In seconds Robbie was shredding it, and Tig was practically hopping like a rabbit behind her drum set, excitedly keeping the rhythm fast and hard. Olivia's arrangement was fierce, but Tig had practiced with Lee and with her phone enough times that she was able to keep pace without being distracted by what the other musicians were doing. Kyra kept up fairly well, even on the first run-through, and Claire didn't need any time to warm up—she brought it on the first note.

When the song was over, the girls stared at one another in silence for a moment. "Were we really just as good as I think we were?" Tig asked.

"Woo!" Robbie shouted, throwing a fist in the air. "It's good to be back!"

Not to say that there weren't a few kinks to work out. Kyra took pointers from Robbie without complaint, and they mic'd everyone but Tig to do backup vocals. Even as well as things were going, she was still a little spooked about trying to sing when the weight of keeping the tempo for the whole band rested on her shoulders. The last thing she wanted was a repeat of Kyra's party. Better safe than sorry.

The next few run-throughs were even better. The vocal accompaniment on the chorus gave their cover more depth.

"We sound good!" Kyra said.

"I know," Olivia agreed. "But it needs something."

"Olivia's right," Tig said. "Technically, we've got this. I mean, sure, we've flubbed a few notes here and there, but for our first group practice, I'm beyond stoked. Another week and a half of practice and we'll have it. But like Olivia said, something is missing."

"What, Tig?" Claire asked. "What do we need?"

"Showmanship," Tig said.

Robbie nodded.

"One more time from the top," Tig said. "As soon as I set this up." She went to the door of the studio and turned her phone to record, propping it up so she could video all of them at once. Then she made her way back behind her drum kit and counted off.

After the song was over, the girls crowded around Tig and watched the video. They looked wooden. Claire was gripping the microphone as if she were hanging on for dear life. Tig could barely be seen, but she knew a close-up would reveal her counting with her mouth as she played. Kyra and Olivia stood there like cutouts. The only one who seemed to be having any fun at all was Robbie, but even she seemed inhibited. "I don't want to be the only one rocking out," she said.

"Regan actually did us a favor today," Tig told the girls.

"By insulting us and calling us losers?" Kyra asked.

"Yes, in fact," Tig said. "Kyra and Robbie were making the same point about image. But when Regan said it, I guess it made me think about how harshly people judge a band based on things that have nothing to do with the music. I've been so worried about our sound that I hadn't even given a second thought to how we look. Even though Regan was just trying to be mean, she was right when she said the only one of us who looks the part is Robbie. Y'all bring your wallets with you?"

They had.

"How much money do you have?" Tig asked.

Olivia had a collection of gift cards from her last birthday, and Claire and Kyra had three weeks' worth of allowance apiece.

"Good. I've saved up a pretty good stash myself. Let's break for tonight and head to the mall," Tig said.

"For what?" Olivia asked.

Tig smiled. "Operation rock star, baby!"

Chapter Forty-Seven

Tig's mom dropped the girls off at the indoor mall, giving them firm instructions to stick together at all times and meet her at the entrance by the department store's shoe department at nine p.m. on the dot.

"Come with me," Tig said to her bandmates.

The girls followed her through the mall, stopping every few stores to try on clothes and accessories. Robbie found Kyra a white leather vest and cuff earrings with spikes and a stack of neon bracelets. "Do this with your hair," Robbie told her as Kyra checked herself out in the mirror at the accessories store.

Robbie pulled Kyra's hair back into a big middle poof.

"Seriously?" Kyra asked.

"Do you want to look like a rock star or don't you?"

"Okay, then," Kyra said.

They finished off her look with leopard shorts, black tights, and ridiculously tall black suede wedges.

For Olivia, they decided on purple jeans and purple heels, a shiny charcoal gray top, and a black fake leather biker jacket.

"Two down," Robbie said. "Two to go."

Getting Claire to give up matching scarves and cardigans took some convincing, but they finally settled on a maroon A-line velvet miniskirt with black tights, a white blouse, and a black blazer. Robbie made it rock with combat boots.

"When in doubt, go with combat boots," she said. "We'll mess up that red hair a little bit and maybe go with a cat eye."

"Oh my," Claire said. "This is different, isn't it?"

"Last but not least," Robbie said to Tig. She took her arm and began pulling her toward a clothing store.

"First things first," Tig said.

Tig took the girls to a salon.

"I am not cutting my hair!" Olivia said. "My tennis coach can't make me, and neither can you!"

"No way," Tig said. "Your hair's so long, it's already a statement. We'll put a knit cap or a fedora on you or—I don't know—maybe a cool headband, and you'll be perfect. So you've got the long hair, Robbie's is black and razored, Claire's is red, and Kyra's will be poofed. So the only one left without a look is mousy, little, shoulder-length me."

"But I have a feeling that's about to change," Robbie said.

"You guys go grab some ice cream or something," Tig said. "I'll text you when I'm done." Tig gave her name to the girl at the counter. There was no wait.

"But, Tig, your mom said for us to stick together," Olivia said.

"Rock 'n' roll is all about rebellion," Tig said. "I'll be fine. I'll text you."

"Tig, these mall places are hit-or-miss," Robbie

said. "What if they don't do a good job?"

"Then it'll just look all the more rock 'n' roll, won't it? Besides, I can't afford anywhere fancy. I have a coupon for this place."

Tig finally convinced her friends to head to the food court without her.

"I'll let you know when I'm done," she told them. "With any luck, you won't even recognize me."

Chapter Forty-Eight

Two hours, three color processes, and one dramatic cut later, Tig was all done. She'd even had just enough time to stop in a shoe store on the way to meet the girls at the food court. They were still sitting outside the ice-cream place.

"What do you think?" Tig asked.

No one said anything for a full thirty seconds.

"Tig?" Kyra finally said. "Is that you?"

"I approve," said Robbie. "One hundred percent."

It was drastic, to say the least. The cut was angled so that it was shorter in the back and longer in the front, and one side was even a little longer than the other. The bottom was choppy, almost as if it had been cut with very large pinking shears. And the color . . . well, Tig was mousy no more. The roots were black, and black lowlights had been worked throughout, but most of her hair was peroxided to a white blond. Here and there, she had hot-pink highlights. To make herself almost unrecognizable, Tig had stopped by the accessories shop and picked up some fake glasses.

The oddest part about it?

Tig looked good.

"That actually really works for your skin tone," Claire said. "I don't know how, and I wouldn't have ever imagined it, but it works."

"You look . . . hot!" Olivia said.

"Really?" Tig asked. "Me? Hot?"

"Smokin'!" Kyra said.

"Kyra," Tig said. "What do you think my mom's going to say?"

"She's probably going to kill you," Kyra said. "But then, you knew that."

"We're about to find out," Robbie said. "It's almost nine. Better head out."

When Tig's mom pulled up in the van, her mouth dropped. "What did you do?"

"I got my hair did!" Tig said, trying to sound jovial. "What do you think?"

"I think you've lost your mind! Let me see you!" Her mother turned Tig toward the crummy lighting in the center of the van's ceiling. "What is this?"

"You'll get used to it, Mom," Tig said.

"I don't understand," her mother replied. "Why?"

"Because, Mom," Tig said, "I'm a rock star."

Chapter Forty-Nine

Tig's dad stared at her so much as she sat at the breakfast table the next morning, he nearly burned the Belgian waffles.

"Tell me the truth," he said. "Did you pierce anything?"

"No, Dad."

"Promise? Not your belly button or— Let me see your tongue."

"Dad," Tig said. "I promise."

"And no tattoos?"

Robbie scoffed. "Tattoos are so last year."

"Well, at least there's that," her dad replied. "So, how does this work? Do you have to pick out clothes now that don't clash with your hair?"

Tig hadn't considered it. "I don't know. Do I, Robbie?"

"Clash away," Robbie said. "It's all rock 'n' roll."

"I suppose there are worse things," Tig's dad said. "But when your grandmother sees you, I don't know you."

"Fair enough," Tig said. "Hey, Dad . . ."

"Yes?"

Tig walked up to where he stood by the waffle iron and whispered so Robbie couldn't hear. "It's not really that bad, is it? I mean, do I look . . . ugly?"

Tig's dad hugged her and kissed the top of her peroxided head. "You couldn't be ugly if you tried," he said. "You'd be pretty even with no hair at all. But don't shave your head, okay? I don't think your mother could take it."

"You look so weird!" her little brother said when he came into the kitchen. "Are you a Power Ranger?"

"Yes," Tig said. "Yes, I am."

He ran to tell their sister the good news.

After the waffles, Tig and Robbie went back to Tig's room to wake the other girls. "Tig!" Robbie said, stopping suddenly. "I just realized that we didn't get an outfit for you last night."

"Covered," Tig said. She took Robbie to her closet, where she pulled out a black tutu with a hot pink hem. "I wore this in my last ballet recital, back in fifth grade," she said. "I figure, we pair it with ripped black leggings and a black rocker tee and these beauties I picked up last night." Tig pulled out of the shopping bag the combat boots she'd bought on her way to meet the girls at the food court. "Like you said, you can't go wrong with combat boots."

"These are spectacular," Robbie said, running her hand along the faux leather. "You are coming along nicely."

After the other girls had breakfast, the band practiced for a couple of hours before their parents picked them up. They sounded better and better with each run-through. Robbie worked on "choreography," teaching Kyra to hold her head to the side and at one point to play with her back up against Robbie's. Olivia could do only so much while playing the keyboard, but she worked on making a fierce face when she joined in to sing backup on the chorus. Claire took instruction on how to do a little hop of sorts before she began singing and how to put her arms up every now and then to get the crowd—not that there would be a real crowd, but still—pumped. She felt ridiculous, but Robbie told her she'd feel less so the more she practiced.

"Own the stage," Robbie told them. "Own it."

Since Tig was already moving both arms and legs as fast as possible, she worked on trying not to do an overbite, which she often did without realizing it. Maybe she'd work on learning how to twirl the sticks before or after the song—something to add a little flavor.

They watched a clip of the real band playing "Submission" to see if they could get any ideas, but Johnny Rotten, their lead singer, cussed a lot and ranted about British politics, so there wasn't much they could use.

"We need to make it our own anyway," Tig said. "How about every day next week we practice for one hour after school? I don't think my mom will go for any more than that."

The girls agreed. When practice was over, one by one, the girls said good-bye. Claire was the last to leave. As she got in the car, she said, "See you at school."

Oh yeah. School.

Tig had been so focused on making the video, she forgot she had to go to school. With this new hair.

That should be interesting.

Chapter Fifty

Walking into the gym that Monday morning wasn't easy. Of course people stared. But Tig noticed that no one laughed. At least there was that.

"That's not helping," Regan said when Tig walked by the Bot Spot. "What? Did you just decide to embrace the ugly? Go all the way with it?"

"No, I just wanted to see if I could look worse than you, but no matter what I try, it's just not possible." Something about the hair emboldened Tig. She felt now that she looked the part of the tough chick she wanted to be.

When it was time for class and everyone was packed in the hallways, Tig heard a man's voice say, "Whoa!" and then an arm stretched out in front of her like a bar, forcing her to stop. It was Coach Cook.

"What is going on here?" Coach Cook wasn't even her teacher. Was he going to hassle her?

"Just something new," Tig said somewhat nervously. She lowered her voice. "See, I'm in this band—"

"You're in a band?" Coach replied. "What do you play?"

"Drums," Tig said.

"Cool." He pointed to himself. "Guitar."

"No way!"

"Way!" Coach Cook smiled. "My hair used to be down to *here*!" He drew an imaginary line with his finger across his bicep.

"Get out!"

"Hair is all part of the package," Coach said. "I dig it. Rock on."

Tig walked away, smiling. She almost ran straight into Will.

"Excuse me. Have we met?" Will asked. "You sort of look like a girl named Anti-gone."

"Go ahead," Tig said. "Take your shots about my hair."

"And the glasses?"

"And the glasses."

"Sorry to disappoint you, but I got nothing," Will said. "I think you look great."

Tig was so surprised, she barely knew what to say. "You do?"

"Yeah," Will said. "But what else is new? I've always thought that." Will gently nudged her toward the door of the computer lab, which was still locked, so that they were standing alone in a little nook while the sea of students flowed past. "I know I've given you a hard time sometimes . . . teased you about stuff . . . but it's only because I think you're fun to spar with."

This was about to go somewhere. Tig could feel it.

She felt her heart flip a little at the way Will's blue eyes shone when he smiled at her. She remembered how helpful he'd been about teaching her drum fills at lunch the past couple of months. She thought about how great he had been to crash and burn with them at Kyra's party, how he'd continued to sit with them at lunch even when he could've easily blamed the whole mess on "girl musicians" and distanced himself from her and the rest of the band in order to hang on to some shred of dignity. But he hadn't. He'd stuck by them. And now he was being sweet, somehow sensing that Tig's whole self-image was at the moment tied into how people would react to her new hair, and he was making her feel good about herself. Because the bottom line was, Will Mason was a great guy. Total boyfriend material.

And Olivia had known it all along.

Tig had to make him understand how she felt.

"Remember what you said a while back, about how girl bands can't work?" she asked.

"I didn't mean that, Tig," Will said. "I was just messing with you. Trying to get a rise out of you."

"You said that girls couldn't be true friends because they're inherently suspicious of and jealous of one another. Always competing."

"Tig, I was just—"

"You made a good point, Will," Tig said. "Girls shouldn't be like that. Friends should have their friends' backs. And that's why I want you to really consider how wonderful Olivia is."

"Olivia?"

"Yes. It's no secret how she feels about you," Tig said. "Olivia is a terrific girl. And one of my best friends."

"Oh. I think I get what you're saying here." Will looked at the floor.

"And I'm really glad you're one of my best friends, too," Tig said.

Will looked up. "I'll always be your friend, Tig," he said. "No matter what."

"So you'll think about Olivia?"

"I'll work on that," Will said. "Just as soon as I'm able to stop thinking about someone else."

Chapter Fifty-One

Someone was definitely thinking about Olivia. But it wasn't the someone Tig had in mind.

"My parents don't want me to do the video," Olivia announced at practice that day. "They don't like the idea of their daughter performing a song by the S-e-x Pistols."

"You do realize we can all spell, don't you?" Robbie asked.

Olivia blushed. "Sorry. My mom won't say that word in front of me. The whole thing makes her very nervous. She wants to know if we can pick another song."

"But we can't," Tig said. "The ad team picked the song because it goes along with the theme of the submarine pants."

"I told my mom that," Olivia said. "She suggested we do the Beatles' 'Yellow Submarine' instead."

"The video is in four days!" Tig said. "We can't learn a whole new song in four days!"

"I already have the sheet music," Olivia said.

"Well," Robbie said, "I can play almost the entire Beatles catalog."

"I know that song," said Claire.

"But Kyra and I don't," Tig said. "Sorry, guys, but we're not quite as advanced musically as you are."

"Is the other song hard?" Kyra asked.

"I don't know," Tig said. "But it's not my decision anyway." She looked at her bandmates. "Fine. I'll call Uncle Paul."

"Absolutely not," Uncle Paul said. Tig had him on speaker. "'Yellow Submarine' is far too obvious. Probably five other teams will do their campaign around it somehow. Can't you just explain that to the girl's mother?"

"We'll try," Tig said.

When they hung up with Uncle Paul, the girls brainstormed.

"I get what your mom is saying," Robbie said. "I, for one, am completely opposed to the sexualization of young girls that the media imposes on our society. But nothing about our video or our rendition of the song plays into that. Right, Tig?"

"No way!" Tig said. "You think my uncle's going to do something gross like that? To his own niece?"

"Maybe your mom could talk to my mom," Olivia said. "She respects her."

"And really," Tig said, "is there anyone more uptight than my mom? I don't think so. If she's okay with it, anybody ought to be."

The girls' next move was to have Tig's mother call Olivia's mother.

As they walked up to the house, Tig looked at Robbie and sighed. "I wonder if Mick Jagger ever had to have his mom call Keith Richards's mom."

Chapter Fifty-Two

Tig's mom winced a bit when they explained the situation to her. "I can see your mother's point," she said to Olivia. "The song itself seems fine to me, but I agree that the band's name is off-putting. So again, I absolutely see her point."

"Perfect!" Tig said. "That's a great place to start the conversation: you see her point. *But—*"

"Settle down, Tig," her mother said. "I'll talk to her, but I'm not going to bully her into anything she doesn't feel right about."

"Mom! Come on!" Tig said. "You've got to help us

out here!"

"All right, all right," she replied. "I really don't think the song is bad at all. Actually, I think it's pretty catchy. It's cute."

Robbie whispered to Tig, "Johnny Rotten is somewhere stabbing himself in the eyeball right now."

The two mothers stayed on the phone for nearly half an hour while the girls paced nervously, throwing out ideas for the worst-case scenario. "We could leave out the keyboard arrangement if we had to," Robbie said.

"Robbie!" Olivia said.

"No offense," she replied. "Just saying."

Tig shook her head, although the thought had crossed her mind as well. There was no keyboard in the Sex Pistols' version, after all. But casting Olivia aside at the first bump in the road was no way to build band unity. "We tried doing a band thing once without the whole band, and look what happened. No. We don't make that mistake again, ever. We're either all in or we're all out." But Tig really hoped they were all in;

she really wanted to make this video.

"And is it just me or do we not love this song?" Robbie asked.

"I do," Tig said. "It's a great song." It had one of the greatest drumbeats she'd ever heard.

Finally Tig's mother emerged from her phone call.

"Well?" Tig asked.

"She said she'll think about it."

The band collectively groaned. "What are we supposed to do with that?" Tig asked.

"I guess you keep practicing until Olivia's mother makes up her mind. She said she'll let you all know her final decision in a day or two."

The girls nodded. . . . What else could they do?

"I'm sorry, Tig," Olivia said.

"It's not your fault," Tig replied. And it wasn't. But Tig hated the fact that the band's fate was held hostage by somebody's mom.

Chapter Fifty-Three

The girls practiced two more days before Olivia's mother gave her decision: Yes. Olivia could play the song in the video.

The band rejoiced. The last practice the day before the shoot was their best yet. They ran through with only a few misses, and those were all Kyra's. Tig was feeling more and more relaxed. There was always the magic of editing.

With thirty minutes to go, the girls decided to do a dress rehearsal. They each changed into their rock star gear and brought full attitude to the last few times through the song.

"This is going to be so awesome!" Kyra said.

"I know! I'm actually having fun!" Claire said. "I don't think I'll even care that people will be filming this. Can you believe that?"

"We rock," said Robbie.

"I'm almost afraid to agree," Tig said. "I feel like I should be a nervous wreck, but strangely, I'm not. I'm kind of Zen about the whole thing."

"No reason you should worry," Olivia said. "Tig, we've got this!"

"Yeah, you're right," Tig said.

Their parents would be picking the girls up from practice any minute. Tig felt that, as the band's leader, she should say something motivational or purposeful in some way to mark the last practice before the video shoot the next day. "Thanks, y'all," was all she could manage to find.

As Tig lay in bed that night, she mentally ran through how it would all go down the next day. Everything was taken care of, from the music to the moves to the clothes to the singing. Nothing had been left to chance.

Everything was perfect.

A little too perfect.

Tig felt unsettled. She wasn't accustomed to things going smoothly.

Any minute the other shoe would drop. She just knew it.

Chapter Fifty-Four

It wasn't a shoe that dropped.

It was pants.

Five pairs of gunmetal gray, slick nylon, high-waisted submarine pants.

With orange suspenders.

"You can change into these in the bathroom down the hall," Uncle Paul said.

Tig stared at him. "You're kidding, right?"

"Why would I be kidding? What did you think, that we were going to advertise a product without actually showing the product?"

"Well, why not?" Tig asked. "You're always saying you love ads that make people think."

"So?"

"So this ad can make people *think* about what submarine pants must actually look like!"

Uncle Paul smiled. "Nice try," he said. "Go put on the pants."

"But we have outfits!" Tig said, gesturing to her and her bandmates' clothing. "Don't we look cool?"

"Absolutely," Uncle Paul said. "Now go look cool in these."

"There is no possible way to look cool in these things," Robbie said.

"Hey, if these stupid pants looked cool, they wouldn't need advertising geniuses to sell them, now would they?" Uncle Paul said. "Shoo. Get dressed."

Uncle Paul shoved the pants at them again. Tig whined and begged, but it was to no avail. He wouldn't budge. Defeated, the girls went into the restroom to change.

"Guys, I had no idea," Tig said.

"We're going to look like complete losers!" Olivia said.

"Yuck! These things make my thighs look huge!" Kyra had already shimmied into her pair.

Claire said, "I would say I wouldn't be caught dead in these, but maybe that would be better than being caught on video. Tig, these really are dreadful."

"Maybe we should just refuse," Olivia said. "I mean, to be fair, no one told us about this part."

Tig had to take control. She thought of Kyra's party and how she'd run away from the band. She wouldn't do that again. Ever. It was time to act like a leader. "Lemons to lemonade, girls," she said. "Let's see what we can do with this."

Kyra's white leather vest covered the orange suspenders, as did Claire's blazer. Robbie pulled Claire's white shirt half in, half out to make the look messy. Tig helped Olivia fit her gray top under the suspenders; Olivia was so willowy, she didn't look half bad in anything. Robbie's look was the least affected, since she had already shown up in leather overalls. The weird pants didn't look that off with her geometric print top and giant statement necklace that covered most of her chest and hung down over the top of the pants.

"Maybe these things aren't so bad," Robbie said. "And hey, nobody else is wearing them, so there's the nonconformist aspect."

"You actually look pretty cool," Tig said to Robbie.

"It's all in here," Robbie said, pointing to her head. "Looking cool is attitude. If you think you look cool, everyone else will, too."

Tig wasn't so sure. She hated to give up her tutu; she'd felt it was a surefire attitude piece in and of itself. Now she would just look like a girl with a weird hairdo and goofy pants.

"A little something for our fearless leader," Claire said. She pulled a wrapped gift out of her bag.

"Aww, Claire!" Tig said. "You shouldn't have!" Tig opened the box. It was a yellow T-shirt that said, NEVER MIND THE BOLLOCKS—HERE'S THE SEX PISTOLS. Tig beamed. "How cool! I love it! Thank you!"

"I thought it would look good in the video," Claire said. "The only thing I was worried about was what Olivia's mom would think when she saw it. Luckily, when you tuck it into these pants, no one will be able to see the band's name anyway!"

The girls laughed. Tig put on the shirt and pants. Strangely enough, the bright yellow against the orange suspenders looked almost like . . . well, like, it had been planned rather than that the pants had been forced on her.

Tig mussed her pink-white-and-black hair in the mirror one last time and then positioned her glasses on her face. "Who's ready to rock this joint?" she said.

The girls gave a collective whoop and emerged from the bathroom.

Chapter Fifty-Five

The ad team had already set up the girls' instruments in front of a green screen. There were a few minutes of light tests and sound checks. The girls were allowed to run through the song once to make sure they were comfortable, then they were told to ignore the cameras and the crew once filming began.

"We're going to record sound and video at the same time," Uncle Paul said. "We don't want to overlay. We want it to sound garagey. If you mess up, just keep playing as if this were a live gig, not a practice. Whenever you're ready."

Tig nodded to Robbie, then to the other girls. She counted off with her sticks. Robbie began shredding the guitar, and Tig furiously banged out the drumbeat. It all happened so fast, and for the most part, Tig wouldn't allow herself to be aware of what the other girls were doing. She wouldn't look away from the drums for fear of losing her concentration, and she completely forgot to guard against the "drummer face" she'd promised herself she wouldn't make. She was vaguely aware that Claire's growl was fiercer than ever and that Kyra flubbed a couple of notes, but Tig just kept banging out the beat as if everything else about the performance depended on it, which it pretty much did.

The song was finished in just over four minutes, but they'd been an intense four minutes. Tig was exhausted.

The college students cheered after the student director yelled cut. "Thank you, girls," he said. "Nice job."

"You can get changed in the restroom if you'd like,"

Uncle Paul said. "You're more than welcome to keep the pants, of course. Our little thank-you gift."

"That's it?" Tig asked. "Don't you want us to play it a few more times?"

"No, we're good."

"But there were a couple of mistakes," Tig said. "Probably more that I didn't catch. And I'm pretty sure I looked bad. I could try to relax more."

"One take," Uncle Paul said. "That's the feel we want the ad to have."

"But, Uncle Paul—"

"Go home," Uncle Paul said. He tousled her hair. "Don't worry. You're a rock star!"

"Can we at least watch the video?" she asked.

"You can see the ad when it's ready."

There was no negotiating. Uncle Paul was never one to second-guess his expertise or let anyone else second-guess it either. He knew what he was doing. Uncle Paul had his vision and that was that.

"Trust me," he added.

The college students volunteered to pack up the instruments while the girls changed.

"That was easy," Kyra said.

"Exactly," Tig replied. It was too easy, just like Tig had worried about.

Tig couldn't sleep that night. As soon as she lay down, it all hit her at once: they'd played their first full song for the public, and Tig knew there had been errors. And they were wearing submarine pants, of all things. And she was probably making a really bad drummer face. And what about the other girls? She hadn't even been able to look at them. Had they looked nervous? Awkward?

This video was supposed to wash away the humiliation of Kyra's party. But no one at school had talked about that in weeks. Maybe the girls should've just let it fade away, but no, Tig had talked them into making a real video to show everyone. But what if this only showed people that Pandora's Box really was just as lame and pathetic as Regan had said? Tig kept coming back to the fact that, no matter what else, they were wearing those ridiculous pants. She wondered if they should've refused to shoot the video, like Olivia had suggested. Tig thought of her "lemons to lemonade" remark that had rallied the girls. What if it had all been a huge mistake and she was to blame for it?

She tried to tell herself no one would see the video. But she knew better. The university's ad team always got local press coverage at competition time. Uncle Paul was kind of a local celebrity for all the wins he'd garnered. Probably the local news would even come out to the school and interview them. Everyone would know. The commercial would be lame, and Tig and the others would be even more unpopular than before. They'd be laughingstocks.

Why? Why had she agreed to make this video?

Chapter Fifty-Six

"I have good news and bad news," Uncle Paul told her when he came by the house two days later.

"What?" Tig asked, not sure she really wanted to know.

"The good news is that the commercial is ready. My students worked around the clock all weekend. We submitted everything by overnight mail this afternoon for tomorrow's deadline."

"What's the bad news?"

"That I lied," Uncle Paul said. "I'm not going to let you see the video."

"*What?*" Tig yelled. "But you promised!"

"I know," Uncle Paul said. "That's why it's bad news. Well, it's sort of bad news. Except that it's not. The reason you can't see the commercial is because it's amazing. It really is. You're going to love it."

"I don't understand," Tig said. "If it's so great, why can't I see it?"

"We're having a huge media event," Uncle Paul said. "After the regional judging, we have a press conference set up where we'll show the commercial. The winning commercial. It will be, Tig. It's beyond good. And we want the band to be there to see the video for the first time along with the press. They want to interview you for your reactions—your fresh, unfiltered reactions. It'll be great!"

"Wait. You're telling me that this video of my band is being shipped off to the competition for other people to see before I even get to see it and then, after that, I don't get to see it until I'm in a room full of people from the media?"

"Yes, I think you have a firm grasp of the situation."

"What am I going to tell the band?"

"Tell them they made a great video and everyone's going to love it."

"But the regional judging won't be for another two weeks! You have to let us see it before you show it to the media!"

"Trust me," Uncle Paul said. "You'll thank me later."

"You can't do this to me!" Tig said. "What if we look stupid? What if I'm making the drummer face? I know I'm making the drummer face!"

"What if you are?" Uncle Paul replied. "We wouldn't have had time to go back and change it anyway. And you girls do not look stupid. The commercial is terrific! You're going to love it!"

"But I know we messed up some places in the song, and—"

"Tig, do you know how long a commercial is? It's thirty seconds. You played the song for over four minutes. You didn't think we were going to use the whole thing, did you?"

CHAPTER FIFTY-SIX

She hadn't thought of that.

"Well, which part did you use?"

Uncle Paul patted her on the head—actually patted her on the head! "You'll see," he said.

Chapter Fifty-Seven

Uncle Paul was right about one thing: two weeks later, the ad won regionals.

The victory party was set for Friday evening at the university. The band, the local media, and all the UA bigwigs would finally see the commercial. Uncle Paul had promised over and over that Tig would not be disappointed. It wasn't that she didn't trust her uncle. . . . Well, not exactly, anyway. She knew he wouldn't purposely embarrass her, and of course she trusted that he knew a good ad when he saw one. But Uncle Paul's concern was simply the ad; Tig's was whether the band had played well. Did the ad show that they knew what they were doing, or would it look staged and faked? Would they look like a real band . . . or like little girls *pretending* to be in a rock band?

"Here's the deal," she told the band at lunch that Friday. Will and Sam were still in the lunch line, so there was no one else to listen. "There's sort of a party tonight."

"A party?" Kyra said much too loudly.

"Shhh!" Tig scolded. "Keep your voice down."

Kyra whispered, "Whose party is it?"

"It's the ad team's," Tig said. "The commercial won regionals."

"We won?" Kyra said, again with too much volume and now with added shrillness.

"Quiet!" Tig said.

"But, Tig, isn't this great news?" Olivia asked. "Why are we whispering?"

"And why haven't we gotten to see the ad yet?" Robbie added.

"That's why we're whispering," Tig said. "I didn't

want to worry all of you, but Uncle Paul refused to let us see the commercial before he submitted it to the competition. He's created a media event where the press gets to see our pure, unfiltered reactions to the commercial at the victory party."

"But what if we hate it?" Robbie said.

"We won't hate it!" Kyra said. "It must be good. . . . It won!"

"That doesn't mean we'll like it," Robbie said. "Maybe it won because the judges thought it was supposed to be a funny commercial. Maybe we look like idiots. Maybe we're a sight gag—like one of those dog wedding memes, with the poodle in a bridal gown and a pug in a tux! Oh man, Tig . . . tell me I'm not a pug in a tux!"

At least Robbie was on her wavelength. "We're not pugs—or poodles," Tig said. "Uncle Paul says we look great."

"Yeah, well—no offense—he's old," Robbie said.

"But the college students aren't," Claire said. "Who knows cool better than college students? Every trend we follow comes straight from them. Am I right?"

She was right. Every next big thing that happened fashion-wise at Lakeview Heights was traceable to somebody's older sister at UA.

"I hope you're right," Robbie said. "I don't want to be a pug in a tux."

"Nobody's a pug in a tux," Tig said. "I'm sure my mom won't mind another sleepover at my house. We can either celebrate after the unveiling or wallow in our misery together. But look, let's not tell anyone about this. With any luck, nobody at school will watch the local news anyway."

"Can I tell Will?" Olivia asked. "He won't tell anyone."

Will? When would she tell Will? Did she mean when he got to the table? Or did they, like, talk outside of school now? And why did Tig even wonder about this? It was her idea for them to talk anyway, wasn't it?

"Well, sure, Will's a vault," Tig said. "He can even come to the party if you want to invite him." Tig meant to be generous when she said it. She wanted to mean it—to be chill about the whole thing. But she sort of wished she hadn't said Olivia could invite Will, and she didn't know why.

"Will!" Olivia said when he and Sam sat down. The next thing Tig knew, Olivia was whispering in Will's ear. It was weird, seeing them so close to each other.

"I'd love to come, if it's okay," Will whispered across the table to Tig. Sam was oblivious, engaged in conversation with the other guys at the bordering table.

"Of course," Tig said. She hoped her smile was convincing. "So it's settled, then. You girls come to my house this afternoon. The five of us will go to the party thing together. Will, we'll see you there."

"Awesome," Will said. "I can't wait to see it."

"Me neither," Tig said. And that, she pretty much meant.

Chapter Fifty-Eight

The party was in the rotunda of the College of Communication. Uncle Paul's students had turned it into a nightclub atmosphere and were blaring dance music and flashing strobe lights. Tig's grandparents had shown up, and both looked a little uncomfortable, plugging their ears with their fingers and grimacing.

The girls had dressed low-key for the event; they didn't want to look too conspicuous if the ad was a joke. Tig wore a knit beanie to mostly cover her hair so as not to draw attention. Some of the students on the ad team hugged the girls and thanked them for helping them create the winning commercial. Tig munched on a piece of celery from the vegetable tray even though she hated celery. The crunching gave her something to focus on besides her nerves.

She saw Will coming up the outside stairs. He was carrying a green cone-shaped paper. As he got closer, Tig could see it was a bouquet of flowers. Her heart did another little flip, like it had the day he'd taken her aside in the hallway. Then she saw him come through the door and receive a hug from Olivia, who'd been waiting for him, and she realized the flowers weren't intended for her. She watched as Will handed the flowers to Olivia, and they hugged again.

"Ladies and gentlemen, may I have your attention, please?" Uncle Paul was in the center of the lobby. "Thank you all for joining us for our victory party! Another regional championship for the UA Department of Advertising!" Everyone clapped. "Next stop, nationals!" More applause. Uncle Paul told the press and the guests about how the competition worked and what the product assignment for this year had been. Then he recognized each team member by name and presented them with certificates. There was a pause as the newspaper photographer took a group picture. "And now, without further delay, please enjoy our winning ad!"

A screen came down over the indoor staircase, and the room went dark again. Suddenly Tig and the other girls were before them all, larger than life, their music playing through the speakers. Most of the intro was gone—Tig's count and the first six bars of the backbeat. Only one bar of the backbeat before the drum fill and then Claire began singing the first line. It was all so fast—wide shots of the whole band, followed by quick close-ups on each girl. They got Claire's little hop, and Kyra looking down sideways at her bass. Olivia was looking to the side and smiling. There was a slo-mo of Robbie tossing her hair back, and Tig's was all flying arms and a quick nod. She wasn't making the drummer face! She actually looked cool for the two seconds the camera focused on her. In between these shots, the wide-angle showed the screen behind them flashing retro-nautical imagery and the words *Submarine Pants* with the name of the store. Before Tig could really process any of it, it was over.

And now people were really applauding.

Tig looked at Robbie. "Were we cool?"

Robbie replied, "Yeah. I think we were."

Tig sighed. "Thank goodness we're not pugs in tuxes."

The lights came back on, and Uncle Paul took his place again. "Please welcome Pandora's Box!" He motioned for the girls to join him. When they did, the newspaper photographer began snapping pictures. Then the TV reporters began asking questions. "How do you girls like your ad?" and "Are you a real band?" and "Where do you go to school?" and finally "Who's the band leader?"

"That would be Antigone Ripley," Robbie said. It was then that Tig realized she hadn't answered a single one of the reporters' questions. She'd been so stunned, she'd left the talking to the other girls.

The reporters began directing questions to Tig.

She thought she answered most of them well enough, but it was all so fast that by the time it was over, she couldn't remember a word she'd said.

"How does it feel to be a famous rock star?" BD asked. He had to yell it over the party music that had started up again.

"My head is swimming," Tig said. "There are so many people here."

"Well, I do know how to clear a room," BD said. "Want me to grab the mic and start singing 'Party Doll'?"

Tig grinned. "No, that's okay," she said. Uncle Paul came over. "Can I see the video again?" Tig asked him.

"Oh, you'll see it," Uncle Paul said. "As many times as you like. My students just posted it on YouTube."

Chapter Fifty-Nine

Someone *had* watched the local news. The video on YouTube was blowing up. Uncle Paul had told her that many of those hits would be the losing teams who'd be watching to see how UA had bested them. He'd warned Tig not to take any negative comments personally: winners had to learn to cope with sour grapes.

Robbie and the other girls had already linked to the page on their social media accounts. The video now had several hundred likes as well as views, and most of the comments were positive.

" 'LOL?'" Robbie asked as they scrolled through

the comments on Tig's computer. "What exactly is that supposed to mean?"

"It means, haters gonna hate," Kyra said.

"Look! This one says 'cute girls'!" Olivia said.

"Is that good or bad?" Robbie asked.

"How can being cute be bad?" said Olivia.

Claire scrolled right past the *Sid Vicious is rolling over in his grave* comment to *The singer kicks butt!* She gasped. "Look, everyone! I kick butt!" she said.

"Here's one," said Tig. " 'I think I have a crush on the guitarist.' Oh, Robbie, you have an admirer!"

"Yours is coming," Robbie said. "It's early yet."

And Robbie was correct. Every girl had at least one admirer by noon Saturday. A few posted that Tig rocked, that Claire killed on vocals, and that Kyra and Olivia were cute. A couple of people said Robbie played like a professional. Several commenters said, *Girls Rock!* and urged the band to stay with music.

At school Monday the girls were practically royalty. People came up to them in the gym and actually asked for their autographs! Tig looked forward to a chance to rub it all in Regan's face, but Regan and her crew refused to look up from the Bot Spot. Tig thought about going up to Regan and saying something smart, but she decided against it. It was enough that she'd proven Regan wrong, and that Regan knew it. Soon Tig forgot all about the Bots and just enjoyed her new celebrity status. The other girls in the band seemed to be enjoying themselves, too: Kyra was positively glowing, basking in the popularity she'd so desperately wanted for so long. Olivia's smile was so big, Tig thought her face must be getting sore. Even Robbie was smiling and laughing with people instead of rocking her usual calculated scowl. And despite the fact that everyone was clamoring for her attention, Claire wasn't even blushing the least bit.

As the first period bell rang and everyone made their way out of the gym to their class, Tig looked at her friends. "What do you say?" she asked. "Practice at my house this afternoon?"

Acknowledgments

Being completely devoid of any musical talent whatsoever, there is no way I could have ever written this book without the help of my many musically inclined friends. I'm sorry I bugged you with so many questions, but I hope when you read this book, you'll think I got it right. If I did, it's thanks to you! Big shout-out to these drummers: my lovely younger daughter; brother-in-law Hansel Stewart; and friends Chris Wier, James Podmore, Matt Wiley, Jud Cameron, Susy Daria; and of course, my dad—the original BD! And for all the other musical assistance, thanks to my sister-in-law Alithea Stewart and friends Michael Terry, Jeff Berry, Justin Brasfield, Kelly Ferguson, Emma Lambiase, and Casie Jones. I admire (and, let's be honest, totally envy) your talent and appreciate your friendship.

Thanks to my former students who inspired this book. Your special gifts and personalities were the pixie dust that helped me imagine many of the girls in these pages. (Rest assured, though, none of you inspired Regan and the Bots!)

Many thanks to Abigail Samoun for being a great friend and a fantastic agent. Thanks for finding the right home for this project.

Thanks to Barb McNally and all the folks at Sleeping Bear Press for loving the Pandora's Box girls along with me and helping bring them to life. Thanks, Catherine Frank, for pushing me to give the girls in these pages my best.

And finally, as always, I thank my family: my parents and brother, who haven't stopped cheering me on since I first wrote my name in crayon; my stepson for reminding me how girls lose their minds over a cute boy; my daughters who inspired Tig's heart and her coolness; and my husband, because, "What is all this sweet work worth/if thou kiss not me?"

About the Author

Ginger Rue is the author of *Brand-New Emily* and *Jump*. She's a former advice columnist for a teen magazine, and her work has appeared in *Seventeen*, *Teen Vogue*, *Girls' Life*, *Family Circle*, and other publications. She is currently a contributing editor for *Guideposts*.

Ginger lives in Tuscaloosa, Alabama, with her husband, two daughters, and stepson. Before she wrote this book, Ginger bought a drum kit and signed up for drum lessons. She failed miserably and has made peace with the fact that she possesses neither rhythm nor coordination. Ginger hopes you like her writing, because there's no hope of her ever becoming a rock star.